THE DEMON'S IN THE DETAILS

NEW YORK TIMES BESTSELLING AUTHOR

J. KENNER

WRITING AS JULIE KENNER

OHB

PUBLISHER'S NOTE: This is a work of fiction. Names, characters, places, and incidents either are the product of the author's imagination or are used fictitiously. Any resemblance to actual persons, living or dead, business establishments, events, or locales is entirely coincidental.

Demon-Hunting Soccer Mom® is a registered trademark of Martini & Olive, LLC. Used by permission.

Published by Oliver-Heber Books

The Demon's in the Details © 2026 Julie Kenner

Cover Design by Dar Albert at Wicked Smart Designs

0 9 8 7 6 5 4 3 2 1

DEMON-HUNTING
SOCCER MOM SERIES

Mommyhood can be hell...

Carpe Demon
California Demon
Demons Are Forever
Deja Demon
The Demon You Know (bonus short story)
Demon Ex Machina
Pax Demonica
Day of the Demon
How To Train Your Demon
The Demon's in the Details

1

———

KATE

’d told myself it wouldn't happen again. For that matter, I'd told Eric it wouldn't happen again. And yet there I was in a cemetery, pinned against a tomb at two in the morning with my dead husband's hands pressing me back against the stone, his lips dangerously close to mine—and my living husband's ring still on my finger.

To be fair, the situation wasn't quite as scandalous as it sounds. For one, Eric isn't actually dead anymore. Well, technically, his body is dead and buried, but his soul has taken up residence in the very alive body of David Long, a former high school chemistry teacher turned fellow Demon Hunter.

So while the man currently pinning my wrists above my head might not look like my first husband, he's not a rotting corpse. Far from it, actually, since David's the kind of dreamy teacher who'd been the subject of many a student crush.

For another, this isn't a romantic encounter. This is work. Or it had started that way. We'd gone out just before midnight to follow up on a lead about a nest of demons set up in an apartment complex near the beach. We'd found the nest. And, yes, it was full of demons. To be precise, the nest had been comprised of six demons who—as the self-described leader told us—weren't interested in that "whole rampagey scene." On the contrary, these demons wanted only to chill.

More specifically, they wanted to chill with gummies and old episodes of SpongeBob.

We could have killed them just for being useless, but when you got right down to it, who among us had never gotten sucked into the dramatic allure of Bikini Bottom? So, much like a benevolent cop, we'd given them a pass, then decided to take advantage of being out to do some training.

That's how we'd ended up in the cemetery behind the Greatwater Mansion. As for how I'd ended up with Eric pinning me tight? Well, that's my own damn fault. We'd been running scenarios, with me playing the role of hunter and Eric playing the somewhat ironic role of demon. I'd sworn I wouldn't let him catch me, but I screwed up and ended up trapped. And the fact that my heart was now pounding, and my breath was becoming more and more shallow had absolutely nothing to do with forbidden desire and everything to do with these impromptu training exercises.

Really.

My name is Kate Connor, and I'm a newly promoted Level 7 Demon Hunter with Forza Scura, a secret arm of the Vatican tasked with hunting demons and other nasties. I used to be a stay-at-home mom to my teenager and my preschooler, but that life went haywire several years ago after a demon burst through my kitchen window and pulled me back in from retirement.

I'm still Mom, and I still stay at home, but now I'm the headmistress at Forza's California-based, first not-on-site-at-the-Vatican school for Demon Hunters in Training, and home is the spooky old mansion overlooking a cemetery that serves as Forza West.

Eric and I had met and grown up together in the original Forza training center hidden deep under the Vatican, and it's both an honor and a still somewhat terrifying reality that I'm now in charge of training the next generation.

That, however, is not my immediate problem.

"Yield," Eric said, his warm breath tickling my ear.

I tilted my head back to meet his eyes, then pushed forward. I saw raw heat light his expression and felt that familiar wave of delicious tension cut through me.

"Kate," he murmured.

"Eric," I whispered at the same time as I hooked my ankle behind his knee and twisted hard to the left, an action that broke his grip and sent us both tumbling onto the damp grass between the Whitmore family plot and a crumbling angel who'd seen better days. We rolled twice before I ended up on top, my forearm pressed against his throat.

"You were saying?"

He grinned up at me, not even slightly concerned about his compromised position. "I was saying that you fight dirty. I like it."

I smirked. "I fight to win. There's a difference."

"Is there?" His eyes searched my face in the moonlight. "I guess that depends on what you're trying to win."

I pressed harder against his windpipe. "We're sparring, David. Not philosophizing." I used his new name as a reminder—to both of us—that we are no longer a couple. His whole dying thing—and my second marriage—had firmly put the kibosh on that. Well, except for that one little fall off the wagon...

In one quick move, he grabbed my hips and easily flipped me, reversing our positions with the kind of move that would've made Marcus—the head trainer at the school—assign me hours of extra defensive practice. Because now Eric was the one on top, his body aligned with mine in a way that felt victorious on a number of disturbing levels.

"Definitely not philosophizing," he said in a soft murmur. "This is something else entirely." His lips were so close to my ear I felt the tickle of his breath all through me.

"Get off me," I said, my voice shakier than I wanted.

"Make me."

I could have. We both knew I could have. A sharp knee to the groin, an elbow to the temple, a strategic bite if things got desperate. But I didn't move, and that was the problem, wasn't it? That was the whole damn problem.

"Eric." His name came out half-warning, half-plea. "Don't."

"Don't what?" He lowered his head, his lips brushing my ear. "Don't tell you the truth? Don't remind you of how good it felt being together last year?"

I shook my head. "That was a mistake, and we both know it." Last school year, my husband Stuart had been in a coma-like state after throwing himself into the middle of a demonic ritual to save my and Eric's daughter, Allie, from being taken over by Lilith, a seriously dangerous demon who—at least for now—seemed to have disappeared back into the ether to lick her wounds. Hopefully, she'll stay hidden under her covers for at least a century. God knows, I've had enough of her.

Stuart had been like that for months, but he's come out of the coma now, albeit a bit different. Sure, he's doing a stellar job as the school's Bursar and top admin guy, but when he's not working, he drifts. Sits in a room and stares at nothing. He responds when spoken to, but always with that half-second delay—like he has to come back from somewhere far away just to hear me.

I tell myself it's because the prophetic visions take a huge toll on him, and I believe it. But I also worry about our marriage. Because despite being awake and healthy for months now, he hasn't made a move to touch me and barely returns my kisses. I've called him out on it—and he admits it—but he says he's in "a different place." That it has nothing to do with me, and he's "trying to get his head on straight."

All of which breaks my heart. And which I never, ever, should have told Eric. We'd had one lapse—one—when I'd been certain Stuart would never come out of the coma. It had been warm and wonderful—and at the moment I very much regretted it. Mostly because Eric wants more.

And yeah, so do I.

But it's not happening. It is *so* not happening.

"He's still my husband," I said, giving Eric's chest a shove, but it was a pathetic effort. "The visions are hard on him. You have no idea what it's like to have that kind of thing suddenly thrust on you."

Eric laughed—actually laughed—and the sound vibrated through both our bodies, making me scurry to stand up.

"Katie. Sweetheart," he said, rising, too. "I had a demon inside me for most of my life. I'm living in the body of another man. And I was pretty much controlled—and seduced—by one of the vilest demons to ever exist. Trust me when I say that I sympathize with Stuart. But that doesn't mean I'm conceding his victory."

I crossed my arms and stared him down. "He's my husband. I think that makes him the winner by default."

"I had that title first," he said, taking a step closer.

"And maybe you'd still be cast in that part if you hadn't kept so many damn secrets and, you know, *died*."

He put a finger under my chin and tilted my head up so that I was forced to look him straight in the eye. "Fair enough," he said. "But the competition isn't over."

"It is," I shot back. "And so is tonight's training." I pressed my palms against his chest and shoved him backward.

Atop the cliff on the far side of the cemetery, the spooky

old Greatwater Mansion—now the Forza West Academy—loomed over us, its smattering of lit windows giving it an eerie glow in the coastal fog.

"Kate."

I shook my head. "No. This conversation is over. Stuart is my husband, and he's literally going through hell. I'm not going to leave him."

"Not even if you wanted to," Eric said, and my stomach twisted from the truth buried in those words.

"Maybe we can find time to train again tomorrow before the new kids arrive," I said. "Then we can pick it back up on a daily basis once they're all settled in."

After a forced semi-closure of the school following a harrowing—and educationally disruptive—demonic showdown, we were finally back in business, and the semester would officially start in just a few days.

"He isn't, you know," Eric said, his voice low.

"What are you talking about?"

"Stuart," he said, the tone in his voice making me shiver. "He's not your husband anymore. Hell, he's not even Stuart Connor. Not really. And you know it, too. This world changed him. I know a bit about what that's like."

I shook my head. "He's not you. No one experimented on him. He sacrificed himself for Allie." I blinked back tears. "He doesn't deserve what he got."

"No," Eric said gently, his hands resting on my shoulders. "He doesn't. And what he did for our daughter wins him my unwavering respect. Respect," he repeats. "But not you. I will fight for you, Kate," he added, his voice low. His fingertips brushed a stray lock of hair away from my eyes, and I shivered under the touch.

"It was different before," I said, thinking about that one time I'd given in to desire, and how right it had felt to be in bed with him again. "We didn't think he would ever come out of the coma."

"But we both wanted it." He met my eyes. "We both still do."

"Yes," I admitted because he already knew the answer. "But he needs me."

"Does he? I don't know. But I know I do."

"Stuart didn't sign up for any of this. He didn't grow up in Forza. He wasn't trained. He was just a normal guy who married a woman with a really complicated secret past, and now he's having prophetic episodes that leave him drained and confused and—"

"And distant," Eric finished. "And cold. And completely unavailable to his wife."

"But I'm still his wife."

"You haven't been his wife for a long time. Not really. At what point do we stop calling it an adjustment and start calling it what it really is?"

"Which is what, exactly?"

"Over."

"Till death do us part," I said. "You died, Eric. Stuart didn't."

I expected another argument, but all he did was nod, then brush the grass from his jeans like we'd just finished a pleasant picnic instead of a training session that had been topped by verbal sparring.

"You're the one who screwed up, remember? You kept secrets from me, and they bit you in the ass. You lost, you died, and Stuart won. More than that, he put up with me even after he learned all my secrets. I'm not going to abandon him."

"Maybe." He took a step toward me. I took one back. "But you still want me."

"I've never said otherwise."

"And you showed it to me, too." Another step. Another

retreat. "And not just in bed before Stuart woke up. You show me every time you look at me when you think I don't notice."

"Stop."

"He's not back, Kate. Stuart's awake and walking around, but he's not back. But I am."

A shiver cut through me, because yes, Eric was back. His death may have ended our marriage, but he was still here. Maybe he was in a new body, but it was the same soul. Same memories. Same way of looking at me that made my knees go weak even after all these years.

And yeah, that was all a little confusing.

"He'll get better," I whispered, not entirely sure if I was trying to convince Eric or myself. "The visions will stabilize. I've talked with Father Corletti.

"Father Corletti said he's never seen anything like it." Eric's hand came up to cup my face. "If he said anything, it was priest-speak for 'I have no earthly idea what's happening to your husband, and I don't want to tell you that he might be losing his mind.'"

I shook my head. "No. Stuart's going to get through this."

"Katie." His thumb traced my lower lip, and I shivered despite myself. "Stuart may get better. I hope he does, for Timmy's sake if nothing else. But even if the visions stabilize, even if he figures out how to live with whatever's happening in his head..." He paused, letting the words hang between us. "He may never be the man you married. Not anymore."

I pulled away, needing distance, needing air. I ended up leaning back against the tomb, hugging myself to ward off the chill from the nearby ocean.

"It'll be okay," he said, his voice gentler now. "Whatever happens. It'll be okay."

"You don't know that."

"No. I don't." He reached out, taking my hand in his. "But I know that I'm here. And I'm not going anywhere." He lifted my hand to his lips, pressing a kiss to my knuckles. "I'm still me, Kate. I'm still the man you married. Different body, same soul. Same love."

"You're not," I said.

He didn't argue. He just leaned in and kissed me.

And because I'm apparently incapable of making good decisions where Eric Crowe is concerned, I kissed him back. Just for a moment. Just long enough to remember exactly why I'd fallen in love with him all those years ago in the Forza training rooms deep beneath the Vatican.

Then I shoved him away and slid back into a sparring stance, because that was safer. That was something I knew how to do. "We're supposed to be training."

"Then show me what you've got." He mirrored my stance, circling left as I circled right, the tomb between us.

I feinted left and struck right, but he was ready for it, blocking my punch and using my momentum to spin me around. I countered with an elbow to his ribs, and we separated, both breathing hard.

"You're pulling your punches," he said.

"I'm not trying to actually hurt you."

"Why not?" He grinned, that infuriating, irresistible grin I knew too well. "Afraid you don't have the stomach for it?"

I lunged at him, and the game was definitely on. We weaved around the tombs and tombstones, trading blows and blocks, neither of us quite willing to commit to a finishing move. It was less like combat and more like dancing—which, knowing Eric, was probably exactly his point.

He caught my wrist on a particularly sloppy punch and used it to pull me close again. "Admit it," he murmured against my hair. "You want more than training sessions."

"Sure," I said, my breath shallow. "I want world peace and no demons."

He laughed, then turned that into a feint and lunged. I

spun, but tripped over a branch, stumbled a few feet, then tripped over something solid and wide. I went down hard, the odor of burnt flesh filling my nostrils.

"Eric," I said, and he went perfectly still. The man knows my voice well.

"What is it?"

I fumbled in my back pocket for the penlight I keep there, but Eric had gotten to his first, and now he aimed it at the ground. More specifically, at the dead man on the perfectly trimmed grass.

A man I recognized.

A man who shouldn't be here.

Antonio Russo. A man who'd been coming here from Rome to join the staff at Forza West as Marcus Giatti's assistant trainer.

"What the hell happened?" I whispered as Eric took my hand to help me up.

At first glance, there was nothing. No wounds, no blood, no obvious cause of death. Just that odor. Antonio could have been sleeping, except for the unnatural stillness and the way his eyes stared at nothing.

Then Eric swept the penlight lower, and we both saw it.

There, on Antonio's palm, burned into the skin like a brand—a symbol. Angular lines intersected with curves, forming a pattern that seemed to be entirely random.

"What the hell is that?" I asked.

Eric made a sound low in his throat.

I whipped my head up to look at him. "You recognize it?"

"It's a *Signum Fidelis*," he said, his voice tight.

I shivered. That really wasn't good. A *Signum Fidelis* is a demon's unique signature, and demons usually don't sign their work. On the contrary, the mark ends up on a victim only when the demon wants to leave a very, *very* clear message.

In other words, this was what we Demon Hunters call a Really Bad Thing. "Do you know which demon?"

"Not off the top of my head," Eric said. "But I'll text the image to Father Corletti and hit the books myself, too."

"Why kill Antonio?"

Eric met my eyes. "I don't know."

I trembled, my mom instincts now on overdrive. "Let's go," I said, already moving. "I want to check on Allie."

2

ALLIE

I pretty much melted as Jared kissed me slowly and thoroughly, like we had all the time in the world. Which, I suppose, he did.

His lips moved on mine, his tongue teasing, soft and sure and sweet. And for once, I wasn't thinking about demons or my strange new life. This was notable because I was almost always thinking about demons. More specifically, about demons and me and prophecies and freaky occult stuff.

All an occupational hazard of being the girl who closed the gates to Hell. The engineered product of a demonic and human bloodline. The Chosen One who prophecies talk about in that ominous, capital-letter way that made me sound like a comic book character instead of an almost seventeen-year-old who still couldn't manage to parallel park.

But right now, at two in the morning with the mansion quiet around us and Jared's tongue teasing mine as his hands slid under the hem of my t-shirt, demons were the absolute last thing I cared about.

His fingers traced up, moving over my ribs, his skin cool

against mine. His body temperature ran a few degrees lower than human, which, honestly, was kind of nice on warm California nights. I arched into him, deepening the kiss, and felt him smile against my lips.

"You really should be sleeping," he murmured.

"You really should be letting me sleep." I pulled back just enough to look at him. In the dim moonlight filtering through my blinds, his features were all sharp angles and shadows—high cheekbones, a deliciously sexy jaw line, and dark hair that fell across his forehead in a way that made my fingers itch to push it back. He had the kind of face that belonged in a black-and-white photograph, timeless and a little bit devastating.

"You started it," he said, the tease clear in his voice.

"I absolutely did not."

"Trust me," he said. "You did. You rolled over and put your leg across mine." His hand settled on my hip, his thumb tracing lazy circles through the thin cotton of my sleep shorts. "That's starting it."

"That's called getting comfortable."

"That's called starting it." He kissed the corner of my mouth. My jaw. The spot just below my ear that made my breath catch and my toes curl. "I've been alive—well, more or less—for almost a hundred and thirty years. I know when someone's starting something."

I laughed despite myself. "Okay, grandpa. Tell me more about the olden days."

He nipped at my earlobe—gentle, no fangs—and I squirmed against him. "Respect your elders."

"You look seventeen."

"I was almost eighteen when I was turned, thank you very much. And I can pass for all the way into my twenties. Maybe higher if I dye my temples gray."

He stretched out, then propped himself up on one elbow, looking down at me with those dark eyes that have witnessed more than a century. His expression managed to be both ancient and boyish at the same time—the weight of a hundred-plus years softened by a crooked smile that still made my stomach flip.

I leaned in, then brushed my lips over his.

He flashed that grin I love—and that my best friend Mindy calls *movie star devastating.*

"I'll have you know that in my day, a young lady would never be so forward."

"In your day, a young lady would have been married off at sixteen to some guy with a good cow."

"That's a gross oversimplification of nineteenth-century courtship rituals."

"But not entirely wrong?"

"Not entirely." He ran his finger through my recently highlighted brown hair, long enough now that it falls almost to my breasts. I should have cut it by now—there's nothing more annoying than a demon who's a hair-puller in a fight. But Jared likes it long. And I liked the way he was playing with it now, letting the strands slide between his fingers like he's soaking up the sensation.

"And yes," he said, clearly fighting a grin. "Cows were definitely a factor."

"I love it when I win," I said, pulling him to me. In one smooth motion, he shifted, straddling my legs and leaning forward, and this time the kiss was slower, deeper, the kind of kiss that made time go soft around the edges. His hand slid from my waist to my breasts, his fingers cupping them, and I made a sound I probably should have been embarrassed about.

We'd been doing this for a while now—Jared spending nights in my room when I couldn't sleep, which lately was most nights. It had started innocently enough. He rarely slept. I couldn't sleep. It made sense for him to keep me company.

But somewhere along the way, *keeping company* had

evolved. First, it was just talking in the dark, his voice low and steady, grounding me when my thoughts spiraled. Then it was talking while he held me, my back against his chest, his arms wrapped around me like armor. Then it was holding me while I fell asleep, my head rising and falling with his breathing—unnecessary breathing, but he did it anyway, just for me, just so I'd have something to ease me into sleep. Then I'd drift off, listening to the silence where a heartbeat should have been.

Somehow, that silence had become the most comforting sound in the world.

I don't know what finally gave me the courage—maybe it wasn't even courage, maybe it was just need—but one night I'd lifted my head and kissed him. We'd kissed before, sure. But not in bed. Not wrapped in the intimacy of night clothes and pillows and unspoken desire.

He'd kissed me back. And it had been awesome and felt devastatingly right. So very, very right. New, but familiar, too. Like I was discovering something I already knew by heart.

And it wasn't just that he was perfect on paper. Because, okay, yeah, he was. I mean, considering who and what I am, a normal boy probably wasn't ever in the cards.

A normal boy wouldn't understand why I spent my afternoons training with knives instead of studying for the SATs. A normal boy would freak out if I told him I'd bled on an ancient stone to seal a gate between dimensions. A normal boy would run screaming if he knew that I carried demon essence in my blood—not possessed, not controlled, just…tainted. Different. And powerful enough to make me the only person on the planet who could close certain doors. Or open them.

Jared didn't run. Jared had been there when I was first trying to figure out what all of it meant—when I was terrified and overwhelmed and convinced I was going to get everyone killed. He'd told me I was strong when I felt anything but, and somehow, coming from someone who'd survived over a century of darkness, that had meant something.

My friend first. My boyfriend second. The emphasis had always been on the friend part, even as the boyfriend part kept growing, kept wanting more.

We hadn't gone further than this, though. Not because I didn't want to—I definitely, definitely wanted to—but because Jared was annoyingly noble about the whole thing. Something about wanting to do things right, respecting me, blah blah blah. Very old school of him.

Also, my mother's a Level Seven Demon Hunter who could literally kill him, and my dad's a resurrected Demon Hunter who could also literally kill him, and even my stepdad had developed some weirdly freaky prophetic abilities that might give him advance warning of any deflowering attempts.

So, yeah. There were practical considerations about the whole relationship thing. And definitely about the sex thing.

We had the relationship. I wanted the sex.

As if he was reading my mind—which he assures me he can't do—Jared pulled back, both of us breathing harder than necessary—well, me breathing harder, but I could tell he was as worked up as I was. I met his eyes and saw that same desire. For a moment, I wanted to beg, but then he settled onto his back and pulled me toward him, and good sense returned.

I curled into his side, my head finding its familiar spot on his chest. The cotton of his t-shirt was soft against my cheek, and beneath it, nothing. No heartbeat. Just stillness and the solid presence of him.

"You're thinking again," he said, his voice a low rumble I felt more than heard.

"How can you tell?"

"Your heartbeat. It's doing that racing thing it does when you spiral."

"That's creepy."

"That's vampire." He pressed a kiss to the top of my head, lingering there like he was breathing me in. "Talk to me."

I stared at the ceiling. Moonlight cut across it in pale stripes through the blinds, painting silver lines on the plaster. Tomorrow—well, technically today—the new students will arrive. Three kids who'd be joining Ren and Ana and Mindy and Eliza. Three kids who'd probably heard stories about me.

"The new students," I said. "They'll know who I am. What I did."

"The gate."

"Yeah. Last year, Bruce told everyone when they first got here, and everyone at *Forza* knows. Now it's become this whole legend. *The girl who closed the gates of hell.* Like I'm some kind of superhero."

"You kind of are."

"I'm really not." I shifted so I could look at him, propping my chin on his chest. In the moonlight, his face was all planes and shadows, beautiful in a way that sometimes made it hard to breathe. "It's just...being a teacher. Having them look at me like I have answers. What if I screw it up?"

Jared was quiet for a moment, his fingers trailing absently up and down my arm, leaving goosebumps in their wake. Then he said, "You taught last year, and it went fine."

"Hello? Do you remember last year?"

"One bad apple." Jared shrugged. "And you handled it. Been there, done that."

I wanted to argue, but he had a point. We'd stopped Lilith, which is saying a lot.

"I still wouldn't call it fine," I say. "But I get your point. Doesn't make me less nervous."

"Your fears are just noise, Al." He shifted to look at me properly, the humor draining from his face. "You are extraordinary. Hell, you threw yourself at Lilith without hesitation. You closed the freaking gates to hell. And you make seriously awesome chocolate cupcakes."

I had to laugh. Then, tear up a bit when his expression turned serious again, and he took my hand.

"You don't freeze," he continued, his voice rougher now. "Not when it matters. So, stop worrying about whether you'll be good enough for some kids who are lucky to learn from you, and start trusting yourself the way I trust you."

"That was a very good speech."

"It wasn't a speech. It was the truth."

I blinked back more tears, then reached up and traced the line of his jaw. Sharp. Perfect. Frozen at seventeen for over a century, and he'd continue to look exactly like this long after I was dust. That was the thing, wasn't it? The thing I tried not to think about too much.

He was going to look seventeen forever. And I wasn't.

I thought of *Highlander*, a movie mom had foisted on me supposedly as entertainment back when I'd first gotten the hots for Jared. She wasn't wrong to warn me, because the man I've fallen for isn't going to age. But I will. And I know most almost-seventeen-year-olds don't tend to dwell on mortality, but the whole demon-hunting heritage kind of changes that. And the truth is, that movie will be my future if Jared and I stay together. I'd watch him stay frozen at seventeen while I turned eighteen, twenty-five, forty, sixty.

He'd stay beautiful while I got wrinkles and gray hair and eventually died, leaving him alone again.

"Where'd you go?" Jared asked softly, his thumb brushing across my cheekbone.

"Nowhere." I forced a smile. "Just thinking about how you've had time to practice everything. Kissing included."

"That's not where you went."

Damn vampire perception.

He was quiet for a long moment, then he sighed and took my hand. "We don't have to figure that out tonight."

"I know."

"We don't have to figure it out ever if you don't want to. We can just..." He trailed off, and for a moment, he looked almost vulnerable. A century-old vampire, uncertain. Because of me.

"Just what?" I asked.

"Just be. For now. For as long as we want."

I nodded, fighting a fresh wave of tears, because he'd given me the perfect answer. I didn't want to think about forever right now. I just wanted to think about this. About him. *Us.* About the way his hands felt on my skin and the way he looked at me like I was something precious, something worth waiting a hundred years for.

"Yeah," I said. "I like the sound of that." I bit my lip. "Do you know what else I like?"

A sexy grin tugged at the corner of his mouth. "Tell me."

"Kissing."

He didn't need to be told twice.

This kiss was different from the earlier ones—deeper, more urgent, like we were both trying to outrun something. His hand slid up my back, pulling me closer until there was no space between us, and I tangled my fingers in his hair. It was softer than it looked, thick and dark, and he made a low sound in his throat when I tugged on it that did interesting things to my nervous system.

"Allie," he murmured against my lips. Warning and wanting, all wrapped up in two syllables.

"I know." I whispered. "Me, too."

His body pressed against mine, solid and cool through the thin fabric of our night clothes. My fingers found their way under his shirt again, tracing the muscles of his back—muscles I'd watched in action during countless training sessions, sparring with him until I was breathing hard and he was a little less controlled than usual.

He shuddered—actually shuddered—and I felt a surge of power, liking that I could affect him like this. That I could make a century-old vampire lose his composure.

"You're dangerous," he murmured against my collarbone, his lips cool and soft against my heated skin.

"I'm a Demon Hunter. Dangerous is in the job description."

"That's not what I meant."

I knew what he meant. And it thrilled me more than it probably should have.

"You're beautiful," he said, pulling back to look at me, and there was something raw in his voice that made my chest ache.

"No fair. I can barely see you."

"Vampire vision."

His eyes glinted in the moonlight, and I wondered what I looked like to him—hair probably a mess, lips swollen, cheeks flushed. "That's creepy," I teased.

"That's vampire."

I laughed, then tugged him closer for another kiss.

"It's late," he said, his lips brushing mine as he spoke.

"I'm wide-awake."

He laughed into the kiss, and I swallowed the sound, wanting to keep it. Wanting to keep this moment, this feeling, this impossible thing tight against me, safe where I could never lose it.

His hands slid up my sides, leaving trails of heat despite their coolness, and I shifted so I was more on top of him than beside him. Somewhere in the back of my mind a voice pointed out that we were supposed to be sleeping, but the rest of my mind told that voice to shut up and go away.

My shirt was riding up. His hands were everywhere. And I was just thinking that maybe tonight would be the night we stopped being so damn responsible when my bedroom door flew open.

And Mom stood there.

For one horrible, frozen second, nobody moved. Then Mom's eyes went wide—taking in me on top of Jared, both of us rumpled, my shirt twisted halfway up my torso, his hands frozen where they definitely should not have been when my mother was watching. Then his hands were gone, moved so fast I hadn't even seen it happen. Vampire reflexes. Too bad they hadn't kicked in earlier.

"I—," Mom started, then stopped. She turned her head, looking very deliberately at the wall. "I should have knocked. I'm sorry."

I scrambled off Jared so fast I nearly fell off the bed, yanking my shirt down. "Mom. This isn't—we weren't—"

"I really don't need details." She was still staring at the wall, her jaw tight. I noticed that she had dirt on her clothes and her hair was escaping from its ponytail, and there was a leaf stuck near her temple. She'd been in the cemetery with Daddy—training, they called it. And I had to wonder if maybe they'd been doing what I'd been wanting to.

"Defcon 3," Mom said. "Get downstairs."

And then she was gone, the door swinging shut, her footsteps already retreating down the hall.

I stared at the closed door, my heart pounding and my face burning.

"Well," Jared said, and there was a hint of amusement in his voice that made me want to throw a pillow at him.

"Don't." I grabbed my hoodie from the chair and yanked it on, as if covering up now would somehow undo what she'd already seen. "Just don't."

He was already on his feet, calm and composed, like he hadn't just been caught with his hands up my shirt. "Defcon 3 isn't that bad. You could handle Defcon 3 in your sleep."

"I'm not freaking out about Defcon 3!" My voice came out higher than I intended. I took a breath, trying to get myself under control. "I'm freaking out about my mother walking in on us."

"It'll be okay. Kate likes me."

I shot him a look as I shoved my feet into my sneakers. "Maybe not anymore."

3

———

KATE

I was not going to think about it.

The Greatwater Mansion's spooky halls stretched before me, all polished wood, marble, and shadows, the high windows letting in just enough moonlight to navigate by. I paused at Timmy's door out of habit, then cracked it and listened to the soft rhythm of my little boy's breathing and, faintly, Fran's voice from the attached nursery, singing Elena back to sleep. My almost-five-year-old was safe with my friend-turned-nanny, dreaming of rockets and dinosaurs, blissfully unaware that something terrible had happened in the cemetery outside.

I closed the door softly, then continued down the hall, wishing I could be blissfully contemplating dinosaurs instead of—

Nope. Really not thinking about it.

The mansion had once belonged to Theophilus Monroe, a descendant of San Diablo's founding family with an unfortunate obsession for the occult. I could feel that history in the bones of the place—in the strange symbols inlaid in certain floor tiles, in the way shadows seemed to gather in corners even when the sun was blazing outside. And in the spooky library that had come with the place, full of dark occult books filled with things I've neither seen nor heard of—and that says a lot.

My best friend Laura had once compared the mansion to the hotel from *The Shining*, and she wasn't wrong.

Tonight, at nearly three in the morning, the comparison felt even more apt. I headed down the grand staircase, then hurried along the corridor toward the sitting room even as my mind kept trying to veer back to what I'd seen when I'd burst into Allie's room. Her shirt twisted up. Jared's hands. Alli—

Not. Thinking. About. It.

I had bigger issues. Like, oh, the demon who'd killed Antonio.

That's what I needed to focus on. Not the fact that my still sixteen-year-old daughter was clearly further along in her relationship with her vampire boyfriend than I really wanted to think about. Not the mortifying moment of eye contact with Jared while my daughter scrambled off him like the bed was on fire.

Murder.

I needed to focus on the much less confusing problem of murder.

The sitting room doors were open, warm light spilling into the hallway, and I could hear the low murmur of voices. They'd gathered fast—I'd sent Eric to rally the adults while I'd gone to splash some water on my face before getting Allie.

That was something, I suppose. Better to have me walk in than her father.

Still, lesson learned. Always. Knock. First.

I paused in the doorway, taking in the scene—my best friend Laura in her pajamas, perched on the sofa arm next to Cutter, who looked grim and alert and ready for action despite the hour. The man could go from dead asleep to fully operational in seconds. Former Navy SEAL thing, I guess. They don't live at the school, but they keep rooms here for convenience—like when we're about to welcome new students.

Eddie was in his ancient flannel robe, looking exactly like an ex-Demon Hunter turned curmudgeonly pseudo-grandfather. Which, of course, he is.

Stuart took the recliner, leaning back in sweatpants and a Rolling Stones tee.

He barely looked my way, and I blinked back a fresh wave of tears as I shifted my attention to my cousin Eliza. She was sitting cross-legged on the floor near the fireplace, her dark blonde hair pulled back in a messy ponytail, watching me with those sharp eyes that reminded me so much of Allie. Technically, she's a student. But she's also an adult and family, so it made sense for her to be at this meeting.

As for Eric, he stood leaning against the wall, his expression grim. He nodded, a silent acknowledgement that he'd moved the body, tucking it somewhere safe from coyotes and other evidence-eaters.

As for Allie, neither she nor Jared had arrived yet, and my mind was spinning about what exactly they might be doing.

As if they'd timed it, the subjects of my angst burst past me into the room—Allie in a hastily thrown-on hoodie and sweatpants, Jared trailing at a respectful distance with the kind of perfect composure that only someone who'd been alive for over a century could pull off after getting caught with his hands up a girl's shirt.

Neither of them met my eyes. Or each other's, for that matter. Allie dropped onto the loveseat, and Jared settled beside her. I caught his eye as they got situated. He had the grace to look slightly abashed, but still took Allie's hand with his own.

I had to give him points for that.

Bigger issues, Kate. Much. Bigger. Issues.

On that firm reminder, I ran my fingers through my hair, then moved to stand by the cold fireplace, crossing my arms and trying to project calm authority while my mind drifted to the memory of Antonio's body and the *Signum Fidelis* burned into his hand.

"Well?" Eddie grumbled, his gray hair standing out in all directions, giving him the look of a mildly crazed eighty-something curmudgeon. Which, frankly, was exactly what he was. "And it better be good, Katie-girl. I was in the middle of a very nice dream about Rita."

His wife, Rita, was away on a trip with friends. Since Eddie hadn't wanted to stay in their empty house—technically, my and Stuart's empty house—he'd decided to camp out in his old room at the mansion for a few days, leaving Kabit, my displaced cat in the temporary care of my old neighbor—and suburban arch-nemesis—Marissa.

Fortunately, Kabit can get along with anyone bearing kibble.

I turned to Eric, half-expecting him to tell the others what happened. He didn't, of course. I'm the headmistress of this school. This was my news to deliver.

"Eric and I found a body in the cemetery tonight." I let that land before continuing. "Antonio Russo."

The reaction was immediate. Laura gasped. Cutter's jaw tightened, his hand moving instinctively to Laura's back. Eliza sucked in a breath. Stuart's head came up, something flickering behind his flat, emotionless eyes.

Allie leaned forward, her fingers interlocked with Jared's. "I trained with him," she whispered, blinking back tears. "Those weeks at the Vatican after the gate thing. He was the nicest guy."

Jared released her hand, and she wiped away tears as his

arm slid protectively around her. And right then, a little piece of my Mom Angst fell away.

"Why was he even here?" Laura asked. "He's not supposed to arrive until late tomorrow, sometime after Marcus gets here with the new kids."

"No idea."

"Does Marcus know yet?" Cutter asked.

I shook my head. "I didn't want to give him news like this over the phone—not when he's got three new students to shepherd. He needs to be focused, not grieving." I swallowed hard. "I'll tell him when he arrives."

"What happened?" Eddie's voice was gruff. "How'd he die? Demon attack, assume. But how?"

I glanced at Eric. "There were no obvious wounds. No signs of a struggle. I only realized his neck was broken when I moved the body. But there was a mark—a symbol burned into his palm."

"His *palm*?" Allie repeated as Cutter asked, "What kind of symbol?"

"A *Signum Fidelis*." Eric pushed off from the wall. "A signature mark. Most demons don't sign their prey, but this one did. Frankly, I'm wondering why."

"But that means you know which demon did it, right?" Laura asked.

Eric shook his head. "Not yet. We'll have to research the symbol. But one thing is clear," he added with a quick look at me. "Whoever this demon is, he wants us to know who he is and that he's here."

"Well, that's never good," Eddie said, in the world's biggest understatement.

"But why?" Allie asked. "I mean, why would any demon want to point his finger at himself?"

My eyes met Eric's, and I shrugged. "We don't know. Not yet, anyway."

"Why was Antonio here early?" Stuart's voice was hoarse, but steady. More like himself. And I felt a tiny ping of hope that he'd taken another step toward a full recovery. "If he wasn't supposed to arrive until tomorrow, why was he in the cemetery tonight?"

I shrug. "Whatever the reason, someone made sure he never made it inside. I don't think it was as simple as a demon thinking we didn't need two combat instructors."

"Maybe Antonio was bringing a message," Laura said. "And someone made sure he never delivered it."

I nodded. "Could be."

"An urgent message," Cutter added. "Why else would he come early?"

"You're not wrong," I say. "Except it could be a dozen other reasons, too."

"I went back and moved the body to the Monroe mausoleum," Eric said. "And I put in a call to Forza. A team will arrive tomorrow to take his body back to Rome." He drew a breath, his shoulders carrying the weight of grief. "We may have a lead," he added, pulling a small USB drive from his pocket. "I found it on Russo. Nothing else. Not even a wallet."

"What's on it?" Allie asked.

Eric shook his head. "I tried, but couldn't hack the password." He crossed the room and handed it to Laura. "Give it a go?"

"Sure," she said, her eyes as wide as if she were looking into an oncoming train. "But I'm more research gal than hacking gal."

Eric's mouth twitched into a grin. "Get Mindy to help," he said, referring to Laura's daughter, who had a knack for computer stuff.

"My kid, a hacking whiz," Laura said. "Makes a mother proud." She glanced around the room. "Seriously, though, it might take a while. If we succeed at all."

Eddie's scowl deepened, but his voice was quieter than usual as he turned to speak to me. "Russo was coming from the Vatican, right?"

I shook my head. "No. He'd been traveling all over the globe. A vacation before coming here. His plan was to show up tomorrow evening."

"I just texted Father Corletti," Eric said. "He's going to see if he can identify the mark." I sent him a pic from my phone. He didn't recognize it offhand, either."

From his place in the recliner, Stuart made a sound like the air being forced out of his lungs, and it made every hair on my body stand up.

I turned just in time to see his eyes roll back—and to hear the long, low howl that burst out of him like the ominous wail of a warning siren.

4

KATE

"*S*tuart!"

I was moving even before I finished saying his name, catching him as he started to slide sideways in the chair. His body had gone rigid, every muscle locked, and his eyes, when they rolled forward again, were white. Completely white. No iris, no pupil. Just endless, milky nothing.

"A vision," Eric said, though we'd all figured that out on our own. After going head-to-head with the high demon Lilith to save Allie, this had become a regular—albeit disturbing—thing.

"Kate," Eric added gently, "you should give him some space."

But I couldn't back off. This was my husband, and I knelt beside the chair, one hand on his arm, and watched as his mouth opened and words that weren't his slipped out.

"The door will bleed."

Stuart's voice, but not. Deeper. Older. Like something ancient was using his throat as a megaphone.

"The door will bleed," he repeated as his body shook and

tremors ran through him like electricity. *"Only living shadows can seal the wound. Blood calls to blood."*

I tightened my grip on his arm, not sure if I was willing him to come back or to tell us more.

It didn't matter. His body went limp, and I caught him before he could slide out of the chair. I pulled him against me and felt the reassuring thud of his heart hammering against my chest. "Stuart. Stuart, can you hear me?"

His lids fluttered open, and I looked into eyes that were familiar again.

"Kate?" His voice was soft and thready. "Another?"

I nodded. "Do you remember?" When he shook his head, I added, "You said the door will bleed. Does that mean anything?"

"Nothing."

"How about only living shadows can seal the wound?"

His brow furrowed, his lips moving as he repeated the words, then slowly shook his head.

I forced a smile and nodded. "Well, that's okay. It's over."

It wasn't, though. Not really. There was something there. Some sort of truth hidden in these strange words that left him hollow and drained. But I didn't have a clue what that truth was.

That was frustratingly normal—or what passed for normal with Stuart's visions. The prophecies came through him like water through a pipe, leaving him empty and drained on the other side. Sometimes he remembered fragments. Usually, he remembered nothing. But I never discounted them. After all, his prophetic words had saved us all from one of the vilest demons ever to inhabit hell. Not to mention this world.

I looked around the room at the others. Laura had gone pale, and Cutter had moved even closer to her. Eddie was frowning so hard his eyebrows had become a single fuzzy caterpillar. Eric's face was carefully blank, but I could see the tension in his jaw.

And then I caught it—a look passing between Eric and Allie. Quick. Loaded.

"Well, ain't that a pisser," Eddie said, apparently understanding what I, too, had just figured out.

"Living shadows," Allie said as she looked around the room. "Me and Daddy."

"What?" Laura said. "No."

Allie nodded. "We're alive. The demonic essence in us is the shadows."

Laura whipped her head around to face me. "Yeah," I said, resigned. "Already got there."

"And we'll deal with it," Allie said, her voice firm, but her hand so tight in Jared's her knuckles were white. Still, her chin lifted in that stubborn tilt I knew so well. She wasn't going to fall apart. She wasn't going to run. She was going to face this head-on, whatever it was, because that's who my daughter had become.

My heart cracked a little more, right down the fault lines that had formed every time this life had asked too much of her.

The silence stretched as we all sat with the weight of those words.

"Do you know any details?" Allie asked Stuart, even though she knew perfectly well what his answer would be. We all did.

"Sorry, kidlet," he said, sounding miserable. "I'm just the damn messenger."

She made a sweeping motion with her hand. "Well, it doesn't matter until we figure out what we have to do. I mean, it's hardly news what me and Daddy are."

She wasn't wrong.

"So we need to focus on Antonio," she continued. "Some

demon killed him in our backyard. We need to find out who and why."

My kid was right. We could spiral about prophecies later. Right then, we had a murder to solve and a message to decode.

"I should write it down," Stuart said. "The damn things never stay in my head."

"I remember it," I said. "I'll write it down. You need to rest."

"I'm fine."

"Stuart."

"I'm fine, Kate." There was an edge in his voice I'd been hearing more often lately. The edge of a man who was tired of being treated like he was broken. Fair enough, I suppose. Except that most of the time, he was still acting broken. Staying locked in his room. Sleeping too much. Not seeing Timmy unless Fran or I suggested daddy-time in an insistent sort of way. When we did, they both had fun. But Stuart never initiated, and he used to play with Timmy all the time.

I drew a breath, forcing my heart not to form any new cracks as I said, "I just worry."

He slumped a bit, his voice less acrimonious when he said, "I know. But I've had dozens of these visions. They haven't driven me loony yet."

"I wasn't saying that at all," I said, even though—yes—I was terrified that the visions were harming him on some fundamental level. Now, however, wasn't the time for that conversation. Especially when he had no control over the visions anyway.

I shifted into assignment mode because it was easier than feeling. "Laura, can you poke around online? See if anyone's heard anything about Antonio's movements in the past few days. Weird chatter, rumors, anything."

"On it."

Over the years, she'd built up an impressive network of

contacts in various corners of the internet—hunters, researchers, historians, and a slew of people who knew things they probably shouldn't. It wasn't a formal network—and more than once she'd mistaken the teens in a role-playing game for actual Demon Hunters. But most of the time she came back with solid intel.

I turned to Eric, "Can you be symbol guy? See if you can find the demon who killed him?"

"Done." That was Eric—whatever our complicated history—whatever tension simmered between us—when it came to the work, he was solid.

"I'm going to audit our security in the morning," Cutter said. "We've got three new students coming and a demon bold enough to kill in our backyard. We may not own the cemetery, but we need eyes on it twenty-four/seven."

"Perfect," I said, then turned toward Eddie.

"Already got ears in places you don't want to know about. I'll find what I can find."

I nodded, feeling a bit of weight lift from my shoulders. Then the room began to empty. Laura murmured something to Cutter about wanting a nightcap. Eliza slipped out with a significant glance at Allie. Eric lingered near the doorway, waiting to catch my eye. When he did, the look he gave me said we'd talk later—about the symbol, about what it might mean, about everything we hadn't said in the cemetery.

Allie and Jared were the next to go. She paused at the door, looking back at me with a small smile that didn't quite reach her eyes. "I know what you're going to say. Be careful. Stay alert." Her shoulders rose and fell as she looked at her feet. "Make good choices."

"I was going to say I love you."

She lifted her head, and something softened in her face. "Love you too, Mom."

Then she was gone, Jared trailing after her like a very

attractive shadow. He paused once to tip his head at me, a silent apology mixed with a promise.

I watched them go and tried not to think about what I'd interrupted earlier. Tried not to think about how grown-up my daughter had become. Tried not to think about the prophecy that hung over all of us now.

The door will bleed. Only living shadows can seal the wound.

Whatever that meant, it couldn't be good for Allie and Eric. For any of us, really.

Eddie was the last to leave. He paused in the doorway, fixing me with those sharp eyes that had seen more than I could imagine.

"You okay, girlie?"

"I'm fine."

"Liar." But there was no heat in the word. "I knew Antonio's father back in the day. Good man. Tough as nails." His voice went rough. "The Russos have been with Forza for twenty generations. Hunters, alimentatores, researchers. Good people. Loyal."

He made a gruff noise. "That boy came here to tell you something, and some demon made damn sure he never got the chance." He looked up at me, and beneath that curmudgeonly exterior, I saw real fear. "Whatever demon did this, it wasn't random. Russo wasn't coming just for a visit. He was coming with information. And it got him killed."

"Believe me, I know that." I drew a breath. "Eric and Allie. In the thick of it again." I blinked hard, fighting back tears. "I hate this for her. For both of them, but especially her."

"We all do," Eddie said. "And Jared's on deck, too. Got a tiny bit of demon in him, that boy. Left over from the first vampire. Ancient and minuscule, but enough there to matter." He drew a long breath. "Each of them thinks they're the one, and maybe one of them is. Or maybe it's about all of them." He shrugged as he continued walking, then paused at the door. "Or maybe it's about someone we haven't met yet. Prophecies are tricky like that."

I nodded. "Thank you," I said, my voice almost a whisper.

He chortled. "Hey, I ain't killed the beastie yet."

"For being here," I said firmly. "For all of it."

His curmudgeonly face softened for a microsecond, then his familiar scowl returned. "Don't go getting sentimental on me, girlie. I'm just here because Rita's off on some pansy-ass girl trip." He said it as if he was annoyed, but I knew he was happy for her, off on a trip with old college friends. And, presumably, safely out of danger.

"If it's all the same to you," Eddie continued, "I'm gonna stay until this is settled."

I smiled. "I was hoping you would."

Then he was gone, and I was alone with the cold fireplace and the weight of everything pressing down on me.

But I couldn't rest. Not yet, and I hurried to catch up with Stuart.

"Hey," I said as he approached his bedroom door. The one that should be *our* bedroom.

"You okay? "I asked.

He nodded, but his eyes had that faraway look—the one that told me part of him was still wherever the visions took him. "Just need to sit for a minute. They take it out of me."

I followed him inside. The room was dim, lit only by a small lamp on the nightstand. He settled into the armchair by the window rather than the bed, already more himself than he'd been in the dining room.

"Do you remember anything else?" I asked, perched on the edge of the bed across from him. "About the prophecy? Anything that might help us figure out what's coming?"

He shook his head slowly. "Just fragments. Images that don't make sense. A door. Blood on stone." He rubbed the back of his neck. "It's like trying to hold water. The harder I grip, the faster it slips away."

"It's okay. We'll work with what we have. Maybe—I don't know—make sure we've found every door in this spooky old house and test the thresholds with holy water.

He nodded. "Couldn't hurt."

Silence settled between us, heavy with everything we weren't saying. I watched his profile in the lamplight—the new lines around his eyes, the gray at his temples that hadn't been there a year ago. He looked tired, but not broken. Just...different. Like someone who'd seen things he couldn't unsee.

"I could stay tonight," I said. "In case you have another vision, or—"

"Kate." His voice was gentle. Final. "You don't have to do that."

"I want to," I said. But did I? Or was this guilt talking? Guilt over the feelings I couldn't quite bury for Eric, the man who wasn't my husband anymore? Guilt for dragging Stuart into this life in the first place?

I wasn't sure. All I knew was that I missed my husband. Everything in my personal life was a huge, freaking mess, but I missed Stuart. I missed the man he was. And he wasn't letting me know the man he'd become.

"I know that what happened changed you," I said softly. "And I know that it's hard. But I also know that I don't want to lose you. I need you. And so does Timmy. We love you. And you can move back to the master bedroom anytime."

His eyes locked on mine. "I love you both, too," he said.

I swallowed. "But?"

He rubbed his temples, his eyes narrowing as if the dim light hurt. "I need time, Kate. I need time to figure out who I am again. Hell, I need time to figure out what I am."

"You're a good man. A good father. You're the guy on

deck as the business guru of this school. You're my husband. And I love you."

He nodded slowly, but said nothing, and something in his eyes made my chest ache. For years, he'd seen only what I'd shown him of my demon-hunting life, and that had been exactly zilch. I'd kept it a secret for far too long, keeping him from seeing the real me.

Now, he sees too much. And I have to wonder how much he's seen of me. Of Eric. There was only that one, foolish, desperate time when I'd believed that Stuart was gone forever. But it had been enough to slide Eric back into my heart and my dreams. And my desires.

Did Stuart see that?

Did I secretly want him to? Because then, at least, maybe I'd jar some emotion out of him? Maybe the bland shell that fate and a high-demon had wrapped around him would shatter, and we'd have it out—accusations and secrets and kisses and anger hurled like glass to shatter. But at least it would be there.

But I can't go there now. Not when everything between us is so damn fragile. Not when it might just be my guilt that makes me think that he already knows.

Because if he doesn't, I don't want to tell him. Not yet. Not until he's stronger. Especially since it was just that one time.

"Go get some sleep," he said. "I'll be fine. I've got budget reports to review in the morning anyway. New semester means new expenses."

I almost laughed. Because there he was. The Stuart I'd married, peeking past the shell. Not because he wanted his wife, but his work awaited.

"Fine," I said crisply, and was almost to the door when his voice stopped me.

"Kate."

I turned back.

"We're going to be okay," he said quietly, but with a certainty that surprised me.

"Is that what your visions tell you?"

A ghost of a smile crossed his face—the first real smile I'd seen from him in weeks. "No. It's what my heart says."

I stood there for a moment, caught between wanting to go back to him and knowing I shouldn't. And knowing that he'd probably push me away again, anyway.

Instead, I matched his smile. "Goodnight, Stuart."

"Goodnight, Kate."

I closed the door softly behind me and stood in the dark hallway, pressing my back against the wall, trying to remember how to breathe.

Antonio Russo was dead. A powerful demon was lurking about. We had a prophecy that nobody understood, but that clearly involved Eric, Allie, or Jared. I'd walked in on my daughter in bed with her vampire boyfriend, and three new students would be arriving in less than fourteen hours.

Just another day in my overly complicated life.

But whatever that prophecy foretold, I intended to be ready.

Because Kate Connor didn't play defense.

I played to win.

Especially when my daughter was in the crosshairs.

5

ALLIE

The hallway was dark and quiet as Jared and I made our way down to the dorms, but my head was anything but. The prophecy kept echoing off my skull— *The door will bleed. Only living shadows can seal the wound.*

"You're quiet," he said.

"Can you blame me?"

He shook his head, then lifted our joined hands and kissed my knuckles. "At least you have company this time."

I shot him a scowl. "Yes, it's so much better knowing my dad and boyfriend are in the crosshairs, too. What?" I added when he smiled.

"Boyfriend," he said, his voice full of heat. "I do like the sound of that."

I rolled my eyes, but it had worked. My mood had improved by at least five notches. And then five more when I saw the heat flicker across his expression. "We could just skip the meeting redux with the gang and go back to your room." He bent over and kissed my ear. "You spent so much time decorating it, it's a shame not to thoroughly christen it."

"You, sir, are too transparent."

"Parent being the operative word?"

"Stop," I said, fighting a laugh. "What if my mom's lingering?"

"She'd just think we're enjoying your extra space. I know Mindy approves."

"Of you or my new room?"

He flashed that lust-worthy grin. "Both."

I swallowed a laugh. When I'd upgraded to my own room in the residential part of the mansion, I'd told Mom it made sense because I was doing more teaching than studenting now. But Mindy knew the truth—*Jared*. Because the tiny dorm room converted from servants' quarters that Mindy and I had shared was hardly date-friendly.

And because she's my bestie, she'd assured me that she didn't mind.

Considering how she liked to spread out all her computer gear, I thought she might even have been secretly turning cartwheels about having the room all to herself.

I let my mind drift back to earlier. The way it had felt with Jared's hands on my skin. The way my entire body had seemed to be nothing but want and need.

The way my mom had burst in.

I jumped a little, jarred from my lusty thoughts, and realized we'd almost walked right past the common room.

"Mind elsewhere?" Jared teased.

I brushed a soft kiss over his lips. "Maybe. But don't even think about heading back to my room yet. You know they're all huddled in there waiting for us to give them the scoop."

Sure enough, the entire—albeit small—student body was gathered in the common room. Mindy on the couch with her laptop, my cousin Eliza cross-legged on the floor, and Ren and Ana tangled together on the loveseat, still in that always-touching, new relationship stage.

Jared took his place in an overstuffed armchair and pulled me into his lap as Mindy said, "We heard everything."

"Really?"

She nodded, her newly short, wavy hair was a mess, as if she'd been dragging her fingers through it, and her eyes were bloodshot. For that matter, all of them looked a bit wrung out, and I felt a weird sort of warmth knowing that these guys were here because they had my back—even though I didn't have a clue how they'd heard a thing.

"The study," Eliza explained, probably because I looked clueless. "The door that opens onto the sitting room. We thought it was painted shut, but it's not."

"It was just stuck," Mindy added. "WD-40 fixed it weeks ago."

"And?" I glanced around the room at all of them. "Please tell me you worked some mojo and figured out the prophecy. I mean, it's been at least ten minutes. I expect results from you guys."

"We totally have the answer," Ana said. "You'll kick some ass and save the world." She shrugged. "Because that's what you do."

And the cool—and terrifying—thing was that she actually meant it. Cooler still is the fact that she said it aloud. When Ana first came to the Academy, she was a mousy little thing who'd been sucked into herself after her parents' death and had somehow ended up on Forza's radar. Now, she's grown into a stunningly pretty girl, with real confidence and some pretty kickass fighting skills.

She looked between me and Jared. "You two," she said. "And your dad. You guys are on deck to save the world."

"Again," Ren said with a grin. He'd come into his own on the fighting side of things last year, his lean frame giving him an advantage. Not to mention years of living on the street after his parents had been killed by demons when he was six.

I hadn't known that he and Ana had started seeing each other, but I had to admit they fit.

At that thought, I snuggled closer to Jared, feeling a tiny stir of pain for Mindy—my bestie—and Eliza—my cousin—, neither of whom had somebody at the moment.

"So what do we do about this signature demon dude?" Eliza asked. The leather wrist cuffs she always wore to hide some pretty nasty battle scars caught the dim light as she shifted.

I shrugged. "We do what Mom assigned everyone to do. Laura's checking her contacts. My dad's researching the mark. Cutter's on security. And we wait, I guess. Try to figure out what it means before whatever's coming actually gets here."

"I'm already on the forums," Mindy said, her fingers flying across her keyboard. "At least the ones I visit regularly. DemonSlayer666 is offline, but there are some old threads about signature marks."

"DemonSlayer666," Ana repeated.

"He's very knowledgeable," Mindy said earnestly.

"You're taking demon advice from someone whose only knowledge of demons probably comes from *Buffy* and *Supernatural*."

"They're knowledgeable," Mindy repeated, already typing furiously. "We're not the only ones fighting the good fight."

She had a point, and I had to smile. Even when the world was falling apart, I could count on Mindy to make everything feel slightly less apocalyptic.

"The new kids arrive tomorrow," Ren said. "Anyone else think the timing's suspicious?"

Ana shrugged. "Everything is suspicious now. A butterfly could land on the windowsill, and I'd assume it was a demon spy."

"Demons don't slide into insects," Mindy said absently,

still typing. "What would be the point? They're basically just navigation systems with wings attached."

She was right. Most of the time, demons are just *there*, floating around us in the ether, which is kind of gross when you think about it. But they all want to be human—to experience all those lovely pleasures of the body. I sighed, leaning against Jared. Can't blame them for that.

But because they want it so much, demons keep an eye out and slide into the body of the unfaithful at the moment of death, right as the soul leaves the body. They can—but hardly ever do—take over the body of someone faithful. Those souls fight. And since the whole point is that demons desperately want experience all our human-y emotions, insects aren't exactly on a demon's preferred body list.

"There have been a few recorded instances of demons taking over a hamster," Mindy added. We all just gaped.

"What? It was in the reading for Mom's class last term."

"You actually do the reading for your mom?" Ren asked.

"I do *all* the reading. How do you think I found out about the forums?"

"Whatever, *Hermione*," Ren said. "But seriously, what door was that prophecy talking about? And how do we know for sure it's meant for one of you two?" He looked between Jared and me. "Or your dad," he added, his attention still on me.

I shrug. "We don't for sure. Not yet. And trying to figure out what the prophecy means before we have more information is just going to make us crazy."

"Too late," Mindy said without looking up from her laptop. "I've been crazy since I found out demons were real and my best friend had been fighting them while I thought we were just doing homework and obsessing about boys."

That got a weak laugh from the group. We'd all had

versions of that moment—the before and after that divided our lives between *normal* and *whatever the hell this is.*

"We should try to sleep," I said, even though I knew none of us would. "Tomorrow's going to be brutal."

The group dispersed slowly, everyone drifting toward their rooms with mumbled goodnights. Except for Mindy, who was clearly waiting to chat. Jared lingered, too, his hand still on my shoulder.

"You okay?" His voice was soft.

"Not really. But I will be."

He studied my face for a long moment, then nodded. "I should let you get some rest." He glanced at Mindy, who was making a very poor show of being absorbed in her laptop. "Night, Mindy," he said, before brushing a kiss over my lips.

"Night, Jared," Mindy called without looking up as he swept from the room.

The second the door clicked shut behind him, she closed her laptop and patted the couch cushion beside her. "Spill."

"Spill what? You heard everything."

She fixed me with *that* look—the one that said she could see right through me. We'd been best friends since elementary school. She knew all my tells. "Something else happened tonight. You and Jared? You weren't quite as clingy."

I grimaced. "We're not ever clingy."

"Oh, please. You so are."

She was right. We *so* are. Apparently, tonight I wasn't feeling it. Gee. I wonder why.

"See?" Mindy said, pointing to my face. "You know what I mean."

"Fine. Fine." I plopped onto the sofa, drew a breath, and blurted, "My mom walked in on us."

Mindy's mouth fell open. "No way."

"Way," I said, grabbing one of the throw pillows and hugging it to my chest.

"And, um, what exactly did she see? I didn't think you two had...you know."

"Not that!"

"Well, good. Because I thought we had a pact to share when we did *that*."

"We do," I said. "Maybe." Now that I was edging closer to *that*, I wasn't so sure I'd want to share. That, however, was not the point.

"We were in my room. Making out. And then my door flew open, and there's my mom, and I swear I've never moved so fast in my life."

"Oh. My. God." Mindy was clearly torn between horror and delight. "What did she say?"

"Nothing. Not one word about it. She just told us to get to the meeting." I hugged the pillow tighter. "I think that's worse. The silence. Like she's saving it up for later when she can really let me have it."

"Or maybe she's got bigger things to worry about right now. You know, murder and prophecy and all that. Besides, you're Save The World Girl. You deserve smoochies."

"Maybe." I lifted my head. "But you didn't see the way she looked at Jared. Like she was considering whether she could get away with staking him."

"To be fair, she probably thinks about that regularly."

"Not helpful."

Mindy grinned, tucking her feet up under her. "So... How far did you get? Before the interruption?"

I felt my face flush. "We were just—" I blew out a breath. "Making out. You know. His hands were under my shirt, but we weren't actually going to go further. Not tonight."

"But you want to."

It wasn't a question. And this was Mindy—I couldn't lie to her.

"Oh, yeah," I admitted. "I really, really want to. Is that

terrible? We've been together for ages and I just…I want that. With him. But every time we get close, something interrupts us. Demons, training, my mother apparently having the worst timing in the history of the universe. And Jared being pretty old-fashioned, too."

"Well, I mean, he's old, right?" Mindy said. "So old-fashioned fits."

"I guess so." I looked up at the ceiling and sighed. "This is what my life's going to be like, isn't it? Always a crisis interrupting the good stuff. Always a reason to push things aside. And now, well, what if I never get the chance?"

Her brow furrowed. "What do you mean?"

"This prophecy thing. What if it's really bad?"

"Don't." Mindy's voice was sharp. "Don't go there."

"I'm just being realistic."

"You're being morbid. There's a difference." She was quiet for a moment, picking at a thread on the couch cushion. "I'm a little jealous, honestly."

"Of what? Being the subject of some horrible prophecy? My mom almost catching me topless? Demons the world over wanting to kill me?"

"Of having someone." She said it lightly, but I heard the weight underneath. "You have this gorgeous vampire boyfriend who literally lives down the hall. Who looks at you like you're the only person in the room. Meanwhile, my love life consists of arguing with strangers on Demon Hunter forums."

"DemonSlayer666?"

She stared me down. "He has a very sexy command of demonic terminology."

I laughed, and it felt good—like releasing a valve. "Maybe one of the new students will be cute."

She grimaced. "With my luck, they'll all be trolls. Or worse —cute but boring."

"Statistically unlikely. Three new students, at least one has to be interesting."

"Your optimism is noted and ignored." But she was smiling now.

Outside, the sky was starting to lighten—the first pale gray of pre-dawn creeping past the curtains. We'd been up all night, and the day ahead was going to be brutal.

"Are you scared?" Mindy asked. "About the prophecy?"

I thought about brushing it off. But this was Mindy—my best friend, the person who'd stuck by me through demon attacks and family secrets and all the insanity that had become our lives.

"Terrified," I admitted. "Not just for me. For Daddy, too. Living shadows—that's both of us. Maybe Jared, even though his demony bits are pretty small. And the worst part is..." I swallowed hard. "The worst part is that I almost wish it was just me."

"What? Why?"

"Because if it's just me, I can handle it. I can be brave. I've done it before—sealed the gates, faced Lilith, all of it. But knowing my dad might be in the crosshairs too? That I might have to watch him get hurt, or worse?" My voice cracked. "He's been through so much already."

Mindy's hand found mine and squeezed. "He's tough, Allie. Actually trained and everything. And he's got your mom and Cutter, and Eddie. A whole army of people watching his back."

"I know."

"And you've got all of them plus the rest of us. Whatever this prophecy means, you're not facing it alone."

I turned my head to look at her—this girl who'd gone from normal teenager to demon-fighting researcher in record time. We'd had a couple of rough patches—secrets do that— but in the end, she'd adapted to the insanity with color-coded notebooks and internet sleuthing and a loyalty that still amazed me.

And like me, she was a hell of a lot older than almost seventeen, whether our parents believed it or not. I flashed a grin. "Thanks, Min."

"Anytime." She yawned, finally letting the exhaustion show. "Now go to bed. New kids are coming around four, and we need to look intimidating and competent, not like sleep-deprived disasters."

"Since when are we intimidating?"

"I'm extremely intimidating. I have a spreadsheet for every demon type and their weaknesses. Let's see you match that."

I laughed. "I concede your point."

I headed for the door, expecting to walk back alone, only to find Jared waiting in the hallway.

"Told you he's a good one," Mindy whispered as she passed me on the way to her dorm.

"I heard that," Jared said.

"Damn vampire hearing," she muttered.

"Thanks," he said, but she just kept on walking.

I fought a grin. "You should sleep," I scolded.

"So should you."

"I'm serious. Dawn's coming. Don't you need to...I don't know, find a coffin or something?"

He smiled—that quiet, crooked smile that still made my stomach flip. "You're not as funny as you think you are."

"Moi?" I pressed a hand to my chest. "Of course I am. You're just too ancient to understand my cutting-edge humor."

He laughed, then pulled me close. "I told you. Coffins are a myth. And I don't burn in sunlight. Yet. And I need very little sleep. In other words, I'm fine. You, however..."

He trailed off, and I shrugged. "I'm always fine."

"Liar."

He was right. But what was I supposed to say? That the prophecy had carved itself into my brain and wouldn't stop echoing? That I was terrified—both of dying, and of being the reason everyone else did?

Instead of answering, I kissed him. Soft and slow and desperate in a way I couldn't quite articulate. He kissed me back, his cool hands cupping my face, and for a few seconds, the prophecy didn't matter. The murder didn't matter. The new students and the investigation and the weight of everything pressing down on us—none of it mattered.

Then he pulled back, resting his forehead against mine.

"Remember—whatever this is, we face it together. Okay?"

"Together." I agreed. "Always." Then he walked me to my door, pressed one last kiss to my forehead, and disappeared down the hallway. I watched him go, this impossible boy who'd chosen to love me despite everything.

With a yawn, I slipped into my room, crawled under the covers, and stared at the ceiling, sleep eluding me.

The door will bleed. Only living shadows can seal the wound.

Whatever was coming, at least I wasn't facing it alone.

6

KATE

I stood on the front steps of the mansion, coffee in hand, and my game face on. Three new students were about to arrive, and despite what had happened last night, they deserved a headmistress who had her act together.

Eric flanked me on one side, Cutter on the other. Honestly, we must have looked like the world's most intimidating welcome committee—which, to be fair, we kind of were.

"Smiles, guys," I said. "Let's wait an hour or two before we scare them off."

"Van's here," Eric said, nodding toward the curve in the street.

I straightened, setting my coffee cup on the stone balustrade as the white van turned off the road and into the long, curving driveway. *Showtime.*

The van bore the new Forza West logo on the side—a stylized sword that could pass for an abstract design if you didn't know what you were looking at. Our cover story was a private training academy for competitive fighters and aspiring stunt performers. The kind of place that attracted intense kids with unusual skills. It held up to casual scrutiny and explained away most of the odd things that might otherwise raise eyebrows.

Marcus waved from his spot behind the wheel, then pulled to a stop at the base of the steps and climbed out, scratching his light beard, then stretching after the long haul from the LAX airport pickup. He looked tired, but I saw him go on alert the moment his eyes met mine. I fought a grimace. I really was too easy to read.

Now, however, wasn't the time. Not with the three kids piling out, all blinking in the afternoon sun.

The first was a girl—small, mousy brown hair, hugging herself like she was trying to disappear. Sophie, according to the intake files. Fifteen years old, parents killed in a demon attack on their Iowa farm. She'd survived by instinct and luck and a pitchfork.

The second looked like trouble walking. Trevor. Seventeen, from Seattle. Headphones clamped over his ears, shoulders hunched, and a file that noted he had problems with authority, which wasn't necessarily a bad thing for a Hunter. But it could make training a challenge.

He yanked the headphones down when he saw me watching him, but his expression didn't soften at all.

Zane stepped out last. Dark hair, sharp cheekbones, easy confidence. He immediately moved to help Sophie with her bags, murmuring something that made her smile. Natural leadership. The kind of kid who made everything look effortless—but who might also have an ego to match. You just never knew. The only concrete thing I knew was that he'd fought a mugger about six months ago, survived, and ended up on Forza's radar. The mugger—according to his file—had been a demon that a Hunter had been tracking.

"Welcome to Forza West," I said, shaking each of their hands in turn. Sophie's grip was tentative, Trevor's was clammy and brief, Zane's was warm and firm. "I'm Kate

Connor, the headmistress. Eric and Cutter will show you to your rooms. Orientation begins in one hour."

The front door banged open behind me.

I spun, my hand going instinctively toward a weapon I wasn't wearing, and saw a small blur rocketing across the pavement—my five-year-old on his bike, training wheels wobbling, pedaling furiously toward the van with the determination of a kid who'd spotted something interesting.

"Timmy, NO!" Fran appeared a second later, breathless and apologetic, Elena on her hip. "Sorry, Kate," she said with a grimace. "He heard the van and just took off before I could stop him."

"No worries," I called, already moving, then scooping my son off the bike just before he crashed into Zane's luggage. Timmy clung to my leg, indignant at having his adventure interrupted.

"I wanna see! New friends!"

"Not now, I said, but Zane had already crouched down to Timmy's level, that easy smile on his face.

"Hey there, little man. That's a cool bike."

Timmy stopped squirming, distracted by this attention from a stranger. "It goes really fast."

"I bet it does. You're pretty speedy." Zane glanced up at me, his crooked smile remarkably charming. "Cute kid."

"Thanks." I bent down, then picked up Timmy and deposited him into Fran's waiting arms.

"Come on, buddy," she said, her arms around my reluctant little boy.

"Bye!" he called over Fran's shoulder. "I'm almost five!"

"Bye, kiddo." Zane waved, still smiling.

Sophie waved too, her expression nervous as she giggled. Even Trevor gave a grudging nod.

As Fran carried my son back toward the house, I caught Zane's eye. "He's a cute kid," he said.

"Yeah," I said, feeling more than a little proud. "He really is."

Eric herded them toward the door, and I was impressed when Zane held it open for Sophie, while Trevor slouched through, letting it fall back on Eric and Cutter.

Allie was waiting for them in the foyer in her role as their student liaison, though they'd also come to know her as one of the combat instructors. Ana and Ren were there as well, introducing themselves as they moved in a group toward the dorms.

I leaned against the doorjamb, taking some sort of weird pride in how well this was going. This was only my second group of kids—and last term had definitely gone off the rails —but I had a good feeling that we were due to settle in.

I had, however, seen too much to rely on good feelings alone. But the easy conversation between Allie and Zane gave me hope—and balanced out Trevor's hopefully temporary— but very teenage—moodiness.

On the whole, they were being typical teens, and it felt like they were all going to fit in. That made it a good day for the school, but as I turned my attention to Marcus, I had to shift gears. Because it wouldn't be a good day for everyone.

"Kate?" he said. "What's wrong?"

I waited until the door closed behind the last of them, leaving us alone. Then I readied myself to rip his world apart.

"There's no easy way to say this." I kept my voice steady, even though my heart was breaking all over again. "Antonio is dead. We found his body in the cemetery last night."

Marcus went completely still. "That's not—he's not even supposed to get here until later."

"I know," I said softly. "I'm so sorry."

He swallowed hard. "How? Demon?"

I nodded. "No obvious wounds, no signs of struggle. But there was a *Signum Fidelis* burned into his palm." I held up a hand to ward off his question. "Eric's on it, but he hasn't identified the specific demon yet."

"Antonio called me." His voice had gone hoarse. "Left a message that he'd been doing research and had something important to tell me. I called him back, but just got his voicemail." He drew in a breath, hands fisted. "Dammit, I should have called again, but I was preoccupied with herding kids."

"This isn't your fault," I said. "And we will find the demon who did this. I promise."

He shook his head. "We both know you can't make that promise. A demon can go to ground for a century." He reached for my hand and squeezed it. "But thank you for saying it."

"He was coming early to warn us," I continued. "I'm certain of it. But someone made sure he never got the chance. Which means whatever he found was important enough to kill for."

"If he was coming with a warning, he'd probably have notes. Did you find anything? We need to start digging."

I nodded. That was the thing about Hunters—grief was a luxury we couldn't afford. Not when there was work to do. "We didn't find any documents," I said, "but Eric found his USB drive. We'll start there as soon as he hacks the password."

Marcus nodded. "Right. Okay." He sighed. "I just can't believe this."

"I know. For tonight, you should just rest. And keep this quiet, okay? I'll tell the students eventually—the dangers of the job and all that. But let's let them settle in first."

I frown. "You didn't do a call with him or meet up somewhere on the road, did you? I mean, are the students expecting him to be here?"

Marcus shook his head. "No reason to tell them ahead of time. They knew I'd be their trainer. I figured I'd introduce him at the first session." He rubbed his temples. "Now I guess

I'll need another assistant." He cocked his head. "You up for the job?"

I smirked. "I can stand in when you need me. But I'm going to use my massive powers as headmistress and assign Allie to you."

He nodded. "For working with teens? Can't argue with that."

We'd been walking and talking, but now we stopped at the door. From somewhere inside, I heard Timmy's laughter—high and bright—followed by Elena's squeal and Fran's mock-threatening "I'm gonna get you!" The sounds of a normal afternoon. The sounds of everything I was fighting to protect.

"I'm so sorry," I said again.

"He was a good friend." He reached for my hand. "But so are you."

"Thanks," I said. "I'm so glad you're back for year two."

"You'd be hard-pressed to get rid of me," he said. "We're family, aren't we?"

"Yeah," I said. "We really are."

7

———

KATE

The entrance hall had been designed to intimidate, and it did its job beautifully.

This was the mansion's heart—a cavernous space with gray marble floors and a polished mahogany staircase that swept up to the second level. Floor-to-ceiling windows lined one wall, letting in shafts of afternoon light that the crystal chandelier caught and scattered into dancing dots of color. Normally, this space served as our formal entryway, impressive enough to make visitors think twice about causing trouble.

Today, we'd transformed it into a makeshift assembly hall. Folding chairs had been arranged in neat rows facing a temporary podium we'd hauled out of storage. Behind the podium, Laura had hung the Forza West banner she'd designed last semester—the same stylized sword as our van logo, with our newly-adopted school motto stitched beneath—*In Tenebris Lux. In darkness, light.* Stuart had vetoed my first suggestion, which translated roughly to stab first, ask questions never.

The current students sat in the front row—Ren, Ana, Eliza, and Mindy. The new arrivals had been placed in the row behind them, a deliberate choice to emphasize that they were joining an established community, not starting from scratch.

Sophie sat in the middle, twisting a strand of hair around her finger and looking like she wanted to sink through the floor. Zane flanked her on one side, occasionally leaning over to whisper something reassuring. On her other side, Trevor slouched with his arms crossed and his headphones back on, despite the fact that orientation was about to begin.

I made a pointed show of looking right at him. He made a pointed show of not noticing.

Fine. Maybe I'd address that later. Always nice to end the day reining in a potential troublemaker.

The staff lined the wall to my right—Eric, his arms crossed, ready to teach them both research and demonology. Marcus, still shattered, but holding it together. Cutter, solid and steady as always, with Laura beside him looking eager to dive back in to teaching how best to research all things demonic.

Stuart sat in a chair near the window, clearly tired but present—he'd insisted on attending despite my suggestion that he rest.

Jared stood slightly apart, managing to look both seventeen and ancient at the same time. The new students already knew he was Allie's boyfriend. What they didn't know—yet—was that he was also a hundred-and-twenty-seven-year-old vampire who'd be helping with night training exercises. As for Allie herself, she was seated with the faculty, a nod to her role as both teacher and student.

Eddie had declined to attend, muttering something about orientation speeches being "right up there with root canals and tax audits."

The meeting had an official sort of vibe despite our small student body. But we were aiming to increase the number of students each year, and I figured practice was a good thing.

And speaking of practice... I stepped up to the podium and smiled. "Welcome to those of you who are new, and welcome back to those who are returning. I'm Kate Connor, and I run this school. If you have questions, concerns, or complaints, my door is always open. If you have emergencies, find the nearest adult and start talking."

Sophie nodded earnestly. Zane gave me his full attention. Trevor examined his fingernails.

"Let me be clear about what this place is and what it isn't," I continued. "This is not a summer camp. This is not a reform school. This is not a place where you will learn to do cool tricks to impress your friends. This is the real deal—a training facility for Demon Hunters, and the skills you learn here may one day save your life—or the lives of people you love."

I let that sink in, watching their faces. They all knew the nature of the school by now, but they each had differing levels of knowledge about the supernatural. At the moment, Sophie looked terrified—not surprising considering the demon attack at her home. Zane looked intrigued, and I remembered his file mentioning years of martial arts training, so he should be a solid asset. Trevor had pulled out his phone, which irritated me but didn't surprise me—according to Marcus, the kid had been sullen and closed off for the entire journey, and eye contact seemed to be against his personal code.

"Mr. Dawson." My voice cracked like a whip. "Unless that phone contains critical information about an imminent demon attack, put it away."

Trevor looked up slowly, deliberately. For a moment, I thought he might challenge me.

The room went very still.

Then Zane leaned over and murmured something to him. Whatever he said, it worked—Trevor pocketed the phone with a scowl.

I caught Mindy leaning toward Eliza whispering something behind her hand. Her eyes flicked to Zane, then away—the universal tell of a teenage crush in progress. Great. After everything that had happened in the last forty-eight hours, part of me wished we'd made this a single-sex academy. The last thing I needed was hormones complicating an already impossible situation.

Then again, at least it was normal. Blessedly, stupidly normal.

"The creatures we fight are real," I continued. "They are dangerous. They do not care about your feelings, your back-story, or your potential. They will kill you if they can, and they will enjoy doing it." I paused. "Our job is to make sure you're ready to stop them."

From the way they looked at me, I finally had their undivided attention. I was about to take advantage of that rare state in teens by launching into the orientation material when Stuart made a sound—a sharp intake of breath that slashed through the room. I turned just in time to see his eyes roll back, his body going rigid in the chair.

Not now. Please, not now.

Except, nope. This was very much happening now, as proved by his low moan that sounded like a man in pain.

"Stuart?" I kept my voice calm, but my heart was hammering.

The moan subsided, and his lips moved, but when the words finally came out, his voice sounded older. Deeper.

"The collar hides the teeth."

The new students exchanged alarmed looks, and I heard Trevor's low whisper of "What the hell?"

Then Stuart slumped forward, gasping, and the moment broke.

Trevor jumped to his feet, his eyes wide, and his cool veneer forgotten. "Seriously. What the hell was that?"

I didn't answer, just hurried to Stuart's side and pressed one hand to his shoulder. "Hey," I whispered. "You okay?"

He nodded, already coming back, albeit blinking and disoriented. "I'm fine," he murmured. "What did I say?"

"Nothing important," I lied smoothly. "I'll tell you after." I turned back to the students, summoning every ounce of authority I possessed. "Mr. Connor has a medical condition and has these occasional episodes. Nothing contagious, nothing dangerous, and absolutely nothing to worry about." That was good enough for now. I'd explain about the visions and the battle with Lilith some other time.

Zane was watching Stuart with an expression that suggested he thought I was full of shit. Sophie looked both fascinated and terrified. Trevor had his phone out again, probably posting something on social media.

"Trevor," I said, nodding at his phone, then continuing as he sulkily slipped it under his thigh. "That reminds me—posting on social media about what we really teach at this school is not only grounds for dismissal but will get you a one-way ticket to Rome for the kind of debriefing you really don't want to go through. Plus, everyone in your feed will think you're nuts."

I gave them all my Stern Mom Look, then cleared my throat. "As I was saying," I continued in an *everything's fine here* kind of voice, "this is a training facility. Let's talk about what that means."

I went through the outline I'd used last year at Ren and Ana's orientation—class schedules, dormitory rules, the chain of command, and the absolute non-negotiable requirement to report any demonic activity immediately. I introduced the staff and their roles, getting a chuckle from Ren and Ana when I referenced Jared's specialized skills—and wide, terrified eyes from the new kids. Even Trevor looked unnerved about the idea of a vampire instructor.

"Questions?" I asked when I'd finished.

Sophie raised a tentative hand. "What if...what if we're not good enough? What if we can't do it?"

"Then we'll train you until you can." I smiled and softened my voice. "No one expects you to be perfect on day one. That's why you're here—to learn. The only failure is giving up."

Sophie nodded, looking slightly less terrified. I let my gaze scan the room, lingering for a beat on Trevor. "That said, this is a school, and you are all essentially on scholarship. This isn't juvie. It's not court-ordered probation. You were in the system and got noticed by a Forza recruiter. So we already know you have potential, and I think you'll all fit in."

I smiled before continuing. "At the same time, you're free to walk out that door anytime. Our only requirement is that you keep what we do confidential. If you don't...well, not all demons are unfriendly. And quite a few owe us favors." I added a smile, so they wouldn't know if I was joking or not. I was.

Well, mostly.

"Anyone else?"

Silence. Trevor looked like he had plenty of questions, but none he was willing to ask in front of everyone, and I made a mental note that his surliness might be a disguise for shyness.

I ended the orientation and dismissed everyone to follow Eliza and Ren to the dorms, so they could get settled before lunch. The students filed out, and I noted that when Zane fell into step beside Sophie, he asked her something about Iowa that made her smile. Hopefully, he'd be just as solid with training as he seemed to be with fitting in.

Trevor hung back, waiting until everyone else had left before slouching toward the door.

"Mr. Dawson."

He stopped but didn't turn around.

I stepped down from the podium and walked toward him. "First days are hard," I said. "I get it. New place, new people, new rules. It's a lot."

His shoulders tensed, but he didn't move.

"You don't have to like it here. You don't even have to like me. But you do have to give it a real chance." I moved around so I could see his face. "The skills we teach aren't just about fighting demons. They're about survival. About protecting yourself and the people you care about."

He dropped his gaze, shoving his hands into his pockets. I couldn't tell if he was surly, fearful, lonely, or just scared. Didn't matter. At the end of the day, my job was to get him out of his shell and train him to be a Hunter who could stand on his own or beside other Hunters.

"I'm not your enemy. None of us are. We're just people who've seen what's out there and want to make sure you're ready for it."

He met my eyes for the first time, and for a second, I saw the scared kid underneath all that attitude. Foster care, thick file, bounced around the system. Kids like that learned early that adults couldn't be trusted, and that showing vulnerability could get you hurt.

"Yeah," he said finally with a deep shrug. "Okay."

He walked out, and I let him go. Building trust took time.

Eric passed him coming in. "That one's going to need some extra attention," he said when he reached me.

"Most of them do, one way or another." I watched the empty doorway. "He's got walls a mile high. But there's a reason Forza recruited him. We just need to help him find it."

"You're more patient than I am."

"I'm a mom," I said, then grinned. "Patience is a survival skill."

8

ALLIE

"Okay, verdict time." Mindy flopped onto my bed and grabbed my pillow, hugging it to her chest like a lifeline. "New kid rankings. Go."

Timmy was sprawled on the floor near my desk, crayons spread around him in a chaotic rainbow. Fran had asked if I'd watch him while she and Elena went for a playdate with one of Elena's old preschool friends. At first, Timmy had been at loose ends without his bestie—which I totally got—but he'd finally settled down and had been quietly coloring for the past twenty minutes. I was pretty sure that was a new record for the Rugrat.

"Maybe I should call those world record people," I said to Mindy.

"Careful. You'll jinx us."

She had a point.

I flopped on the bed beside her, then glanced around my room. Last year, I'd been in the mansion's dorm wing—aka repurposed servants' quarters—with the other students. But now, I was back in a real bedroom, with the same furniture I'd had in our old house. And the same pile of training clothes in the corner that I kept meaning to wash. And the same best friend making herself at home on my bed like she owned the place.

So I guess it really is true—no matter how much things change, some things stay the same.

"Hello?" Mindy pressed, snapping her fingers in my face. I smacked them away, and she crossed her arms and scowled. "Hello? Are we ranking or what?"

"What categories?"

She rolled her eyes. "Duh. Hotness. Personality. Overall vibe. Likelihood of being secretly evil." She ticked them off on her fingers. "The usual."

"We have a usual? This is only year two."

She made a clicking sound with her tongue. "I'm adding to last year's spreadsheet."

"Right." I made a show of rolling my eyes as she made a show of shaking her head in mock exasperation.

"You are such a Luddite," she said.

"I have no idea what that is, but I shall proudly wear the crown."

She grinned, and I grinned back. This was normal, at least for us—Mindy's systems and spreadsheets and deep-dives into demon research, me pretending to be exasperated while secretly finding it both impressive and hilarious.

And right now? Well, I'd like a great big helping of normal, please.

"So?" Mindy prompted. "Sophie first. Thoughts?"

I scooted up the bed, then turned to sit with my back against the headboard. The movement made Timmy look up briefly, but he went right back to his drawing without comment.

"Sophie," I repeated, calling up the mental image. Small. Brown hair that hung in her face and a habit of biting her lower lip. "Sweet. A little scared. Reminds me of Ana before she came out of her shell."

"Agreed. Abandoned-puppy energy." Mindy nodded sagely. "She'll be fine once she settles in. This place is weird, but it's good-weird once you get used to it. Trevor?"

That one was harder. I thought about dinner—the way he'd sat at the end of the table with his headphones on, hunched over his food like he was guarding it from predators. The way he'd flinched when Ren accidentally bumped his chair. The flat look in his eyes that substituted for a full-on mask.

"Defensive," I finally said.

"Translation, daddy issues."

"Come on, Min. Leap much?"

She just shrugged. "He's all surly macho guy. Sounds like classic no good male influence."

"You have got to stop reading psych books," I said, but she wasn't wrong. Trevor might as well be wearing a t-shirt that says *The system failed me, and now I trust no one.*

"You agree," Mindy said. "I see it on your face."

"Fine. Maybe you're right." She was, but I couldn't tell her as much since Mom had made me swear not to tell anyone—especially Mindy—that he'd bounced through six foster homes in four years. And that kind of instability left marks. The kind Mom says either kicks you in the gut and knocks you down or makes you strong enough to do the kicking.

It all depends on the kid, and we won't know until we know.

I shrug. "Mom thinks he's got potential."

"Your mom thinks everyone has potential. It's her super-power. She has to. Otherwise, she'd be an idiot to run this school."

She wasn't wrong about that.

"He's kind of cute, though," she said. "In a broody, I-hate-everything way."

"You think broody is cute?"

She shrugged, hugging a pillow tight. "Not cute so much as bad boy hot. And speaking of hot...we're agreed Zane is totally BBH?"

"Don't tell Jared," I said, "but OMG, yes. With his hair and that jawline? Why he's here and not on some sexy streamer is beyond me. And he's nice," I added. Because that's important, too.

Mindy shifted on the bed. "I know, right? You saw him at dinner? He got Sophie to laugh twice, which I think qualifies as a miracle since she looked terrified all morning. Plus," she added, a little breathlessly, " he'd had a pretty solid conversation with Ren and Ana, and he'd even gotten Trevor to grunt in response to a question, which was *way* more than anyone else had managed."

"This could be Fate, Min," I teased. "Maybe he's the Demon Hunter of your dreams."

"I wouldn't shove him away. That's for sure. Plus, he's like the Newbie Whisperer."

I shook my head, completely confused.

"Oh, come on. You saw how he got Trevor to put his phone away during orientation without your mom having to go full headmistress." Mindy clutched the pillow to her chest. "That's like...social superpowers. Which are way better than actual superpowers."

"I don't think they're better than actual superpowers."

She shrugged. "Yeah, well, you have actual superpowers. You don't understand the struggle of us mere mortals."

"You're not mortal. I've seen the crazy magic you do with a computer. I'm pretty sure that's some serious form of witchcraft."

She only smiled serenely.

I twisted around to watch Timmy, who'd stacked up a lot of sheets of paper, all adorned with red rectangles of various sizes. He pushed the current one aside and began a new one, like a preschool Mondrian on crack.

"What are you drawing, Timster?"

He looked up and flashed his best smile. "Doors! Lots of doors!"

I tossed that one around in my head, wondering about deep psychological meanings.

None jumped to mind.

"Why?" I asked.

He shrugged.

Mindy peered down at his work. "You're right, RugRat. That's a lot of doors."

He didn't look up but shook his head. "They're all one door."

"Deep," Mindy said with a grin. "Very philosophical. So," she continued, "Speaking of boys..."

"Subtle much?"

"I'm a master of subtlety." She leaned forward. "Well?" she asked, her voice rising with her brows. "How are things with Jared today? I mean after yesterday's peep show for your Mom? Any awkwardness? With him or Aunt Kate?"

"Will you stop?"

She had the grace to look abashed. "Sorry. It's just, well, it's got to be both mortifying and awesome, right? I mean, you two are like really serious. And I'm living vicariously."

"Fine," I said. "Yes, awkwardness. It'll be a month before I can look at Mom and not blush."

"Did she sit you down for *the talk*. Not the sex one—I remember you telling me about that years ago. But the dating a vampire one."

I shook my head. "No. But she pulled me aside and told me that she knows I'm responsible and she trusts me." I rolled my eyes a little. "We were supposedly talking about the school and me taking on more of the training and all that. But then she added that she really likes Jared and trusts him, too."

"So basically she's heavily guilting you with the truth, but at the same time giving Jared her thumbs-up."

I laughed. "Yeah. I guess she is."

"So are you going to…"

I shrugged. "I don't know. I want to," I admitted quietly. "But at the same time, I don't. I mean, I'm me, you know. This Chosen One demon hunter thing…it's like I got shoved into a grown-up costume and then tossed onto stage and told I had to win the Tony. I mean, I never got to finish being a kid. So, I don't know. I want to—I mean, when we're kissing and stuff, I really, *really* want to. But I think I want to wait even more." I shrugged, feeling beyond awkward. "I haven't told Jared any of that."

"He'll get it. I bet he already does. And besides, it's not like it costs him anything to wait. The guy's got all the time in the world."

She wasn't wrong.

She cocked her head. "Is that weird? I mean, he really does have all the time, and you…" She trailed off with a shrug.

"It's weird," I admitted. "I mean, yeah. What happens in ten years, twenty years, when I start getting older and he…doesn't? When I have gray hair and wrinkles, and he still looks seventeen."

"You could, too, though." Mindy's voice was careful, tentative. But I knew where she was going with this. "If he turned you—"

"Don't tell my mom I said this."

"Scout's honor."

"You were never a scout."

"Semantics. My lips are sealed."

I took a breath, then let it out slowly. "I've thought about it. The turning thing. What it would mean. Being with him forever, never getting old, never having to say goodbye."

"But?"

"But eternity scares me." I stared at the ceiling again, like the answers might be written up there somewhere. "I'm only seventeen."

"Not for a few more days."

"Whatever," I said. "Point is, how am I supposed to know what I want forever? I don't even know what I want for breakfast half the time. What if I change? What if he changes? What if we're perfect now but in two hundred years we can't stand each other, and we're stuck together for all of eternity?"

"That's..." Mindy paused. "Really mature. Plus," she added, "you've got to factor in the whole demon essence thing."

And there it was. The thing I tried not to think about too hard, because when I did, it opened up a whole Pandora's box of questions, and I had no answers.

"Yeah," I said quietly. "There's that."

The demon essence in my blood.

The thing that made me strong enough to seal hellgates and powerful enough to fight things that should have killed me ten times over. The thing that made me special and dangerous and possibly something other than entirely human.

"Would turning even work?" Mindy asked. "With what you are?"

"I don't know. No one knows. There's no precedent for..." I waved a hand vaguely at myself. "Whatever I am. It might work fine. It might kill me. It might turn me into something worse than either vampire or demon." I swallowed hard. "Jared won't even talk about it. Every time I bring it up, he shuts down."

"Maybe he's scared too."

"Maybe." Probably. Definitely. "He told me once that he'd rather have fifty years with me than eternity with anyone else."

Mindy made a sound that was half sigh, half groan. "Oh. Oh, that's like...romance novel good."

"I know."

"I hate him a little bit for being that perfect."

"Same, honestly."

She laughed, and I laughed with her, and for a moment the heaviness lifted. But not all the way. Some things are too heavy to lift completely.

"Allie?" Timmy's voice broke into our laughter. He was tugging at my sleeve, a drawing clutched in his other hand. "How do you spell *for Mommy*?"

"F-O-R," I said, grabbing a scrap of paper from my desk and writing it out for him in big, clear letters. "M-O-M-M-Y."

He studied it carefully, then carried both papers back to his spot on the floor. I watched him copy the letters in the corner of his drawing, his tongue poking out again, brow furrowed in concentration. His handwriting was wobbly but legible. FOR MOMY, it said. Close enough.

"It's a present," he announced proudly, holding it up for inspection. A red door with a gold doorknob, carefully colored inside the lines. "For when she's sad."

"That's really sweet, buddy. She's going to love it."

He beamed at me—that pure, uncomplicated joy that only little kids could pull off—then went back to his crayons, already starting another door.

"Okay," Mindy said, and her voice had that forced-cheerful tone that meant she was deliberately changing the subject. "This got way too serious. We were supposed to be ranking boys by hotness and making fun of each other's life choices, not contemplating mortality and vampire relationships."

"You asked."

"I know, and I have learned my lesson about asking real questions." She swung her legs off the bed and stood, stretching. "New topic. Ice cream. I think there's still some of that chocolate chip cookie dough in the freezer. The good kind that my mom hides behind the frozen vegetables."

"Aunt Laura hides ice cream?"

"She hides everything good. I swear I should make a map." She grabbed my hand and pulled me up. "Come on. Sugar therapy. Doctor's orders."

"You're not a doctor."

"I own a First Aid kit. Close enough."

She was already heading for the door. "Timmy, you want to come? There might be popsicles."

"Popsicles!" He scrambled up, scattering crayons everywhere, and grabbed Mindy's hand.

I gathered up his drawings and stacked them on my desk. The one marked FOR MOMY in his careful handwriting went on top.

"Allie, come on!" Mindy called from the hallway. "That popsicle isn't going to eat itself!"

LATER THAT NIGHT, after ice cream and dinner and the chaos of trying to get everyone to agree on a movie, Jared walked me back to my room.

He hesitated at the door, which he never did. "Maybe I should just say goodnight."

"Don't you dare." I grabbed his hand and pulled him inside. "My mom walking in on us doesn't change anything. We weren't doing anything wrong."

"I know. But she looked—"

"Traumatized? Yeah. Welcome to my world." I shut the door behind us and leaned against it. "She'll get over it. And

I'm not sleeping without you just because she got an eyeful."

His mouth twitched. "An eyeful?"

"Shut up." I crossed to the bed and climbed in, then patted the space beside me. "Mindy's got a crush on Zane," I said. "Did you notice?"

He laughed. "I did. Probably the rest of the class did, too."

I sighed. "Maybe it'll work out. I feel bad, you and me having each other. She needs someone, too."

"She'll find someone. Not sure Zane would be my choice."

I twisted to get a better look at him. "You don't like him?"

He shrugged. "I don't know him. I just wonder how much they'll mesh after she gets tired of looking at him."

I laughed. "Are you afraid I'll get tired of looking at you?"

"You better not."

I snuggled up to him. "Won't ever happen."

He kissed the nape of my neck as he stretched out next to me, one arm draped over my waist. Familiar. Safe.

But even with him there—even with his presence wrapped around me—I couldn't quiet my brain.

Mindy's question kept circling back— *Are you scared*?

The honest answer was yes. But not just about Jared, or the future, or the impossibility of forever.

The truth was, I never used to think about dying. It just wasn't something that crossed my mind. Sure, I knew it would happen eventually—everyone died—but it was abstract. Distant. A problem for Future Allie, the one who was old and gray and had lived a full life. The old Allie didn't waste time worrying about it.

Now I thought about it all the time.

Every training session, every demon we faced, I wondered if this was it. If today was the day my luck ran out. If all the power in my blood, all the training, all the fighting, would add up to nothing in the end.

Jared's arm tightened around me, as if he could sense my thoughts spiraling. Maybe he could. He always seemed to know.

Tomorrow there would be training. Classes. More investigation into Antonio's murder. Tomorrow I'd have to be strong and capable and whatever else people needed me to be.

But tonight, in the dark, with Jared's arms around me, I let myself be scared. Just for a little while.

9

KATE

The new kids had been with us three days now. Long enough to learn which hallways creaked, where our cook, Signora Micari, hid the good snacks, and that Marcus's *light warmup* meant two hours of conditioning that left them barely able to walk.

And, most importantly, they'd learned how to handle a stiletto without injuring themselves or other nearby humans.

And, since I'd spotted an interesting notice in the morning paper, I dropped the bomb at breakfast. "Tonight, we're going on a field trip."

Sophie's fork froze halfway to her mouth. Trevor's eyes flicked up from his plate, the first sign of actual interest I'd seen from him. Zane just smiled, easy and curious, like I'd announced we were getting ice cream.

Out of the corner of my eye, I caught Mindy watching him. That made a total of three times I'd noticed. I'd also noticed that, so far, he wasn't looking back. Frankly, I was fine with that. I was already stressed by my daughter dating Jared. I didn't need to be stressed about Mindy's dating life, too.

I caught Laura's eye and saw that she'd clocked Mindy's

interest, too. She gave me a half-hearted shrug, and I almost laughed. There comes a point when a mom just has to back off. I want to say that I knew that and respected that, but honestly? I was still getting used to the whole growing-up thing.

Fortunately, I liked and trusted Jared. Unfortunately, he had a couple of lifetimes on my kid.

"A field trip?" Sophie's nervous squeak pulled me back to the moment. "Um, you're not talking about a museum, are you?"

"Actually," Allie put in, "there was this one time at the Danvers Museum, and this demon-loving creep named Cool, and—oh," she said, apparently catching my eye.

"Sorry, Mom." She grimaced as she looked at the others. "Later."

We're actually going hunting?" Zane said. "Wow."

Trevor nodded. "Yeah, that'll be cool," he said, in one of his rare statements not prompted by a direct question. "I mean, so long as we don't end up dead."

"That is the plan," I assured them, as Sophie made a squeaking noise. "And you have to get out there sometime. You're here to be Demon Hunters, after all. And the best way to learn is by doing." I passed the breadbasket to Marcus. "Don't worry. You'll have plenty of backup."

"It's actually pretty awesome," Ana said, leaning forward with the enthusiasm of someone who'd survived her first hunt and couldn't wait to do it again. "Scary as hell the first time, but awesome."

"She's not wrong," Ren added. "Remember that alley demon?"

"And you lost your knife and stuck your finger through its eye. That was soooo gross," she added with a shudder as Sophie turned a little green.

"It worked, didn't it?" Ren said, with more than a little pride.

The two of them dissolved into the kind of rapid-fire reminiscing that made the new kids look even more terrified. Sophie went from green to pale. Trevor was gripping his fork like a weapon, which honestly wasn't the worst instinct. And Zane was watching Ren and Ana with what looked like fascination, his head tilted slightly, as if they were everything he aspired to be.

A good sign, actually.

"Breathe," Allie told Sophie. "Seriously. You're going to be fine."

"Says the girl who closed the gates of hell," Trevor muttered.

It was the most words he'd strung together since arriving. Everyone turned to look at him, and I watched his shoulders hunch defensively, like he regretted speaking.

"You're right," Allie said. "Turns out I've got some super-powers. Yay me. But my mom doesn't, and she's the most kick-ass Demon Hunter I've ever met." She turned to look at Marcus. "Sorry about that."

He shrugged. "No argument here."

"We don't know what your skills are," Mom continued, speaking now to the whole class. "But we do know that each of you has potential, or you wouldn't have been recruited. So learn to work with what you've got, and work hard to learn the skills we'll teach. Do that, and you'll be kicking demon ass in no time," she added, making Sophie giggle.

"Remember," I added, "Tonight's just step one. No one's expecting you to do mystical cartwheels."

Sophie put her hand over her mouth to stifle more giggles, then settled back in her chair, apparently realizing we were all staring at her. "What?"

"Well, okay, then," Trevor said, hunching his shoulders

and sounding less surly—and a bit more confident. "I can do that."

"You can," I assured him. "And you will." I looked at each of them in turn. "Wear comfortable clothes and tennis shoes. We'll meet in the Great Hall at dusk."

Marcus followed me into the hallway. "Who's our target?"

I fished the clipping from my back pocket and handed it to him. An old man had collapsed on the beach near the surfboard rental place. The lifeguard said he died, but by the time the paramedics arrived, he was sitting up and talking. They figured the lifeguard just didn't know his stuff, even though he swore the guy had no pulse.

"Gotta be a demon," Marcus agreed as he handed the clipping back to me. But it's been hours. No guarantee we'll find him."

"There never is, but you know as well as I do they like to come back a time or two to the place where he died." I shrugged. "If he's not there, we'll just get ice cream."

Marcus chuckled. "Can't argue with that."

I leaned against the wall. "How's training going? Any thoughts?"

He nodded slowly. "Sophie's still green, but I can already tell she's got it in her. We may not see it tonight, though. I'll keep an eye on her. As for Trevor, the kid's wound pretty tight."

"Tell me something I don't know," I said.

"I think tonight will help. He acts like a surly prick, but I think it's because he doesn't know his place yet. I met quite a few of that type back in Rome. We're still in week one. It'll shake out, I think."

I nodded, thinking about the surly, withdrawn teen, and trying to overlay him with a softer side. "Honestly, I don't see it. But I hope you're right. And Zane?"

Marcus shrugged. "Seems made for the job. Easy-going but

sharp. And strong. He told me he'd done some martial arts training as a kid. He's got potential. I just…" He trailed off with a shrug. "What?"

He shook his head. "Not relevant."

I crossed my arms. "Hello? I'm the headmistress here. What?"

"He just reminds me of one too many smug assholes I've run across. And, no, he hasn't done a single thing that falls in the asshole column."

"He's the kind of guy who'd be the head of a fraternity and the most popular guy in school if he had a different life," I said. "Then again, my only frame of reference for that kind of life is television."

"Yeah, but you're not wrong. His mom died when he was fourteen, but he still managed to stay under the radar. Kept their apartment, found enough work to pay the rent. The guy's a survivor. He's an asset. Not yet, but he will be."

"Agreed." But even as I said it, I couldn't get his situation out of my head. Zane was a boy who'd been entirely on his own, and that kind usually avoids groups—no frats, no community groups. But then Forza called and he jumped. Probably just the allure of the supernatural and the pride of being selected. That's what usually brought in Forza recruits.

But at the same time, a tiny part of me wondered if he'd encountered demons before the fake mugger. Like maybe it was a demon who'd killed his mother.

That could light a fire under a hunter. And a hunter with a purpose was a very good weapon.

THE BEACH near the surfboard rental shop was deserted by the time we arrived. The shop itself had closed hours ago, its cheerful "Catch a Wave!" sign now dark and the racks of boards chained up for the night. Beyond it, the sand stretched toward the water, silver-gray under a half moon.

"Spread out," I said, keeping my voice low. "Stay in your groups. Act like friends out for the night, not Hunters."

They all nodded, then the small mob shifted, breaking into three little gangs. Marcus, Ren, and Ana headed toward the waterline, where the old man had supposedly drowned. Allie took Mindy and Eliza to check out the cafes at the far end of the popular San Diablo boardwalk. And I kept the three new kids with me, steering us toward a nearby taco stand where a few late-night customers lingered over their food.

I'd shown them all the newspaper photo before we left—Harold Messner, seventy-three, bald head, prominent nose. He'd gone swimming three days ago and drowned. Pronounced dead on the beach by the paramedics.

And then, miraculously, he'd started breathing again.

Miracle, my ass.

"There." Zane's voice was calm, almost conversational. He nodded toward the taco stand, where an old man sat alone at one of the plastic tables, working his way through a plate of fish tacos.

Bald. Prominent nose. Souvenir tee he'd probably stolen from a now-dead tourist.

Hello, Mr. Messner. Or whoever was currently wearing him.

"Stay here," I told the kids. "I'm going to confirm."

I strolled over to the taco stand like I was just another hungry tourist, ordered a Coke I didn't want, and took a seat at the table next to my target. He glanced up briefly, then went back to his food.

I watched him pop a couple of mints from a near-empty container, and knew we had our man. Either that or I was hanging with a human who had really bad oral hygiene.

I leaned over, pretending to reach for a napkin from the dispenser on his table. "Sorry—do you mind?"

"Help yourself." His voice was pleasant enough. Normal.

But I was close now. Close enough to catch the smell underneath the peppermint. Faint, but unmistakable—that sickly sweet reek of rot that is a telltale demon giveaway.

I grabbed my napkin and retreated to my table, pulling out my phone to text Marcus and Allie—*Taco stand.*

Then I sipped my Coke and waited.

The thing about newbie demons is they're usually pretty predictable. They've just scored a shiny new body after who knows how long, and they want to enjoy it. Eat good food. Walk on the beach. Maybe find someone to kill or take in a movie, depending on their disposition.

This one seemed content with his tacos for now. But eventually he'd move. And when he did, we'd be ready.

It took about twenty minutes. He finished his food, tossed his trash, and headed down the wooden steps toward the beach. Not toward the lit-up section with the fire pits and the couples walking hand in hand, but toward the dark stretch near the rocks where the shadows pooled thick and black.

All the better.

I gathered my group with a look, and we followed at a distance. Up ahead, I could see Marcus and his students paralleling us along the waterline. At the same time, Allie's group was moving in from the boardwalk side.

We all watched as Messner picked his way across the sand toward a cluster of boulders. Maybe looking for privacy. Maybe looking for prey. Either way, he'd chosen poorly.

We closed in slowly, using the rocks for cover. The moon threw enough light to see by, but the shadows were deep here. Good for hiding...but also good for hunting.

I was maybe fifteen feet away when he stopped and turned around.

"You can come out now," he said, his voice no longer pleasant. "I know you're there."

So much for the element of surprise.

"Spread out," I murmured to my group. "We'll box him in."

We emerged from behind the rocks—me and the three new kids forming one side, with Marcus and his group forming another as Allie's team cut off the way back to the boardwalk. Nine Hunters surrounding one demon.

Those were good odds—at least so long as he didn't have friends lurking nearby.

"Hunters." The demon's smile wasn't the welcoming kind, and the pleasant old man routine had evaporated completely.

"You didn't do your homework," I told him conversationally. There are a lot of Hunters in this town. You would have done better to pick a body in Los Angeles. Nobody would even notice a demon down there." I flashed him my fakest smile, the one I had often used when forced to do something for the PTA. "You should keep that in mind for next time."

The major bummer about corporeal demons is that once they've moved into a dead body, killing them doesn't actually kill them. It just kicks them back to the ether where they can hang out and wait for a new body to slide into all over again.

Only killing a demon in its true form shuts them down completely. Which is one reason you rarely see demons in their true form. Demons really aren't stupid. Plus, in their true form, they're gnarly, scary-looking creatures, and they'd definitely stand out in a crowd.

Fortunately, a demon can't easily slide into the body of someone faithful. That's a good thing, as it really helps to keep the demon population under control.

I made a mental note to quiz the new kids about all of that. But later. Now really wasn't the time.

"Bitch," the demon snarled. "My master knows you, Katherine Andrews. Did you think he would never demand the debt be paid?"

My body went completely cold. I had absolutely no idea what he was talking about. Plus, it was never good when a demon knew your name. For that matter, why did he know my maiden name? I would have still been training, and that was a lifetime ago.

Then again, that was the blink of an eye to a demon.

"Who are you?" I demanded, but he didn't answer. Instead, he moved, and faster than a seventy-year-old body should be able to manage. He feinted toward me, then changed direction, heading for the weakest point in our circle —Sophie. The smallest, and the one he would assume most likely to freeze.

Unfortunately, he would also be right, because that's exactly what Sophie did. She stood rooted to the spot, her eyes wide, her stiletto clutched in a white-knuckled hand as the demon barreled toward her.

"Move!" I shouted, already running—but Trevor got to her first.

I don't know where it came from—the sullen kid who'd barely spoken two words since arriving, the one who seemed determined to hate everything about this life. But when Sophie needed him, something clicked. He threw himself between her and the demon, his body a human shield, his blade coming up in a wild, desperate arc.

It wasn't pretty, but it worked. The stiletto caught the demon across the forearm, slicing deep enough to spray blood across the sand.

Messner howled and recoiled. Trevor stumbled but managed to keep himself planted between Messner and Sophie.

"*Move*," he yelled.

That snapped her out of it. She scrambled backward, grabbing for the weapon she'd dropped. The demon started to lunge again—

And Allie was there.

She came in low and fast, sliding across the sand like she was stealing home plate. Her feet swept the demon's legs out from under him, and he went down hard. Allie was back on her feet before he hit the ground, dancing out of reach with a grin on her face.

"All yours!" she called to the students.

But the demon wasn't done. He rolled and came up snarling—and found himself surrounded—Marcus and me blocking the path to the water, Ren and Ana flanking wide, and Mindy and Eliza near the rocks. Trevor was still guarding Sophie, his jaw set. Zane was right there, too, his stiletto out and his focus on the demon.

Messner's gaze swept the circle, clearly looking for the best way to bolt. His eyes landed on Zane, and he stopped, probably assessing his options. He shifted, his mouth opening as if he was gulping in air or about to shout out for any demonic compadres that might be lingering about.

He never got the chance. Instead, Zane rushed him, crossing the distance like he'd been shot out of a cannon. One second, he was by the rocks. Next, his stiletto was buried to the hilt in the demon's eye.

The demon didn't even get a squeak out as it returned to the ether, and Harold Messner's body crumpled to the sand, empty now, the thing that had been wearing him banished back to whatever hell it had crawled out of.

"Holy shit," Ren said, which pretty much summed it up.

Zane pulled his blade free and wiped it clean on the demon's Hawaiian shirt. When he looked up, he was wearing that easy smile again. "Sorry. It looked like he was going to bolt."

"Nothing to apologize for. That was good work."

"Marcus said to trust my instincts." He shrugged, all bashful modesty. "Saw an opening."

Marcus was watching him with the look of a teacher whose student just aced an impossible test. "Hell of an instinct. We'll work on control, but the talent's there. And the speed."

"Thanks." Zane ducked his head. "I used to run when my life got shitty. So I ran a lot."

"Hopefully it's less shitty now," I said, and he looked down at his shoes. I'd probably embarrassed the hell out of him.

I let myself exhale. The kid was good. Really good. Whatever training he'd had before us had given him skills most recruits would kill for.

"Sophie." I crossed to where she was still sitting in the sand, Trevor hovering nearby.

"You okay?"

She nodded, but her hands were shaking. "I froze. I'm sorry. I saw it coming and I just—"

"It happens." I offered her a hand and pulled her up. "First time's always the worst. What matters is you're still here."

"Because of him." She looked at Trevor with something like wonder. "He saved me."

Trevor shifted, clearly uncomfortable. "Just reacted. Whatever."

"That's exactly what you're supposed to do," I said. "Teammate in trouble, you help. The most important rule in the book."

He met my eyes for just a second, then dipped his gaze down. Not surprising. Most teens didn't like to be in the spotlight. And the ones who did want to be the center of attention tended to cause the most trouble.

"What do we do with..." Sophie gestured at the body, her face pale. "We can't just leave him here, right?"

"We take him back," Marcus said. "Eric handles disposal. We'll talk more about the process in class. Right now, we should get gone before we get noticed."

Sophie looked like she had more questions, but something in Marcus's tone said the topic was closed.

I was grateful for that. Eric's background as a chemistry teacher—or, rather, David Long's background—came in handy in ways I tried not to think about too hard. Some things were better left unexamined.

"As Marcus and I got the body loaded, the new kids clustered together, processing. Sophie kept stealing glances at Trevor—grateful now, not scared. Maybe a little awed.

Trevor ignored the attention. But his shoulders had lost their permanent hunch, and when Zane said something to him, he actually responded with more than a grunt.

Progress.

Allie came up beside me. "That went well."

"It did." I kept my voice low. "Nice slide tackle, and bonus points for not taking the kill."

"Wasn't mine to take." She shrugged. "And they needed it more. Well, Zane didn't—kid's a machine. But Trevor did."

I looked at her—really looked—and felt that familiar swell of pride. "When did you get so wise?"

"I've been taking notes." She bumped my shoulder. "I've had a pretty good teacher. When she's not being annoying."

"I'll take that as a compliment."

"You should," she said as the others climbed into the Forza van. Marcus drove the students—and transported the body. I followed in my Odyssey with Allie. The beach disappeared in the rearview, dark and peaceful again.

Tomorrow would be more analysis. Going over what everyone did right and wrong. But what mattered now was that tonight was a success. Demon dead, new kids initiated, nobody seriously hurt.

More than that—I'd learned quite a bit about the kids. Sophie needed her confidence built, but she had heart. Trevor hid some interesting layers under that sullen exterior, and when it mattered, he'd stepped up. And Zane was everything Marcus predicted. Natural talent, solid instincts. With training, he'd be truly formidable.

"You need to think louder," Allie said. "I can't hear you at all."

"The new kids," I said with a laugh. "I was thinking how they handled themselves."

"Trevor surprised me." She was quiet for a moment. "I mean, he really put himself on the line for Sophie."

"He did."

"And Zane..." She trailed off.

"What about him?"

"Nothing. He's just really good."

"Not everyone arrives as raw as Sophie." I glanced at her. "You were pretty raw once, too."

"Ouch. Low blow, Mom."

"Just saying. Give them time. They'll find their feet."

We drove the rest of the way in comfortable silence, the mansion's lights appearing in the distance like a beacon.

First hunt. First success.

Not too shabby.

"So," I said, when I couldn't take it anymore. "Jared?"

She leaned her head back and groaned.

"I'd convinced myself I wasn't getting *the talk*," she said. "Really, Mom? Do we have to?"

"It's not *the* talk," I said. "It's *a talk*. And, well, yes. Because—oh, hell." I drew a deep breath and started over. Seriously, the parenting thing is so much harder than demon hunting. "You know your dad and I like Jared, right?"

"Well, I knew you did *before*," she said.

I smirked. "Smart aleck."

"Just using humor to deflect the horror and embarrassment. Seriously, Mom, just spit it out. It'll be easier on both of us."

She wasn't wrong.

"We like him," I said. "But it's our job to worry."

"And since you're both overachievers, you worry a lot."

"Well, we do. But," I added, before she could interrupt again, "We also know that you're old enough to make your own decisions. And, well...just remember that it's okay to go slow. At least one of you has all the time in the world."

"Funny. You're a funny mom."

"I'm a mom who worries and who loves you and who trusts you to do what's right for you, whenever and whatever that might be."

"Really?"

I reached across and took her hand. "Yeah, baby. Really."

She wiped away a tear and managed a wavering smile. "I love you, Mom."

"Love you back, kiddo. Always. Just tell Jared that I'll stake him if he hurts you. But not before torturing him first."

She scoffed. "Oh, please. He hurts me, then I'm the one dusting him."

"How about we do it together and call it mother/daughter bonding."

"Oh, yeah," she said. "He'll love it when I tell him that."

I nodded toward her window, where Jared stood waiting. She glanced back at me. "Love you, Mom."

"Love you. Now go."

I'd barely gotten the words out when Allie was out the door, slamming it behind her. She raced to him, and he caught her up and spun her. As I got out of the car, I heard him wish her a happy early birthday. It was midnight. My little girl was seventeen.

Then Jared's arms were around her, and her mouth was on his.

It wasn't a quick kiss. It wasn't shy or tentative or any of the things a mother might hope for when her teenage daughter greets her vampire boyfriend in front of an audience. It was the kind of kiss that said I was worried about you and I'm so glad you're back, and about a dozen other things I probably didn't want to think about too hard.

But it was also a kiss that said *I love you. I'll protect you. I'll always have your back.*

And all things considered, wasn't that what every mom wanted for their little girl?

Behind me, someone giggled. Sophie, I thought. Or maybe Ana.

"Get a room," Ren muttered, but he was grinning.

I stood there by the van, watching my daughter kiss a boy who'd been stuck at seventeen for over a century, and I honestly didn't know what I felt. Pride, maybe, that she'd found someone who looked at her like she was the only thing in the world that mattered. Fear, definitely—the same fear I'd been carrying since the day I learned what Jared was. And underneath it all, something sharper. Something that felt uncomfortably like grief.

My little girl wasn't so little anymore.

Allie finally pulled back, laughing at something Jared murmured against her hair. Her face was flushed, her eyes bright. She looked genuinely, completely happy.

Jared met my eyes over her head.

I gave him a small nod. Not approval, exactly. Just...acknowledgment.

He nodded back.

"All right, show's over," Marcus called out as he walked

back from the side entrance. "Everyone inside. Debrief in ten, then bed. We'll do a full analysis tomorrow."

The students shuffled toward the door, still shooting glances at Allie and Jared, still whispering and giggling. Young love. Drama. The eternal currency of teenagers, even ones trained to kill demons.

I hung back as the others went in, watching Allie say something to Jared—quiet, private, just for them. He tucked a strand of hair behind her ear with a gentleness that made my chest ache.

"He's good for her."

I jumped a mile, not aware that Eric had crept up behind me.

He grinned. "You need to work on not letting things throw you. If I were a demon, I could have had my way with you."

I grimaced at the double-entendre, but otherwise ignored it. "You think so?"

He didn't pretend to misunderstand. "I do. He loves her. He's strong. He's smart. He'll watch her back."

"He's immortal."

Eric sighed. "I know. But she loves him, too. And Kate," he added, "it's her choice. I think she made a good one."

I nodded. The truth was, so did I.

"Oh, hell," I said, tasting the tears that I hadn't noticed. I brushed them away. "Our little girl is growing up."

"She is."

I took his hand. "We did good."

"Yeah," he said, kissing my forehead, "You did."

10

KATE

By the time Eric, Marcus, and I unloaded the body and took it in through the back, I was exhausted. But when we joined the kids in the common room, it was clear that they were still on a high from their adventure—and still dazzled by the Hollywood-style reunion between my daughter and Jared.

Jared.

Eric was right—he really was good for her. So was it horrible of me to wish that she'd fallen for someone else who was good for her? Someone who could move through life with her?

Except that was a stupid reason to wish Jared were a different guy. I adored Jared. Truly. Except for that one little black mark, he was perfect for my kid.

Not only that, but there were no guarantees in life or in love. Anyone could die tomorrow, especially with this life. And if Allie had found her Eric, then I should be jumping up and down and celebrating.

Her Eric.

For a moment, the world stopped turning, and my body

went stone cold. *Eric.* Not my husband Stuart... I'd thought of Eric. More, I'd thought of Eric as my version of what a husband should be. Only not just a husband, but as a lover, a partner, a best friend.

I closed my eyes, and those damn tears came back. I loved Stuart. I truly did. But he didn't check all those boxes. Especially not now. Maybe not even before.

Oh, dear God. I was officially the worst wife in the history of marriage.

With deliberate purpose, I forced my thoughts away from Jared and Stuart and Eric and on to a completely different male—Timmy.

I caught Allie's eye and pointed upstairs as I mouthed her brother's name. Then I slipped out of the sitting room, ignoring everyone else—especially Eric—as I hurried away, keeping my face down, since I was certain that it was painted in broad strokes of guilt and mortification.

I found Timmy asleep in the nursery and decided to leave him there since he was terrible at falling back asleep once he woke up. So I kissed him lightly, then hurried the short distance to the room I technically shared with Stuart, but where he never slept, having claimed another bedroom as his combination office and study. Most nights, I was fine with that. Tonight, I felt like a horrible harpy whose bad attitude and lingering lust for my first husband had leaked out and tainted the universe.

Fortunately, I was distracted from my shame spiral by the crayon masterpieces on my pillow. Eleven pieces of white drawing paper covered with red rectangles, each with two gold dots, one above the other. The note Fran had left with them said that Timmy was still fascinated with drawing doors— which I'd figured out on my own—and that even Elena had jumped on the Door Train and drawn a few.

I laughed, then swallowed, then blinked back tears again

because the thoughts of Timmy had dragged me right back to thoughts of Stuart.

But he hadn't died. Stuart Connor is very much alive. But he's no longer the man I married. It's as if he's living in a tower built of prophecy and visions, and as each day passes, we drift further apart.

I don't know what to do about it.

I'm starting to wonder if I should even try.

Once upon a time, I could talk to Stuart about anything. He'd been my anchor when we'd first met after Eric died. We'd dated, fallen in love, then slid into a normal family existence with Stuart cast in the role of attentive husband, diligent provider, and loving father to his stepdaughter. And, a few months later, to a little boy of his own.

He'd been my husband then, in all possible ways. More, he'd been my friend.

Then demons had come back into my life, and I'd kept silent about my past. And the moment he'd learned that I'd been keeping secrets, it was as if the lock that had been holding our world together had burst, and everything fell apart. We'd put it back together, sure. But instead of that sturdy metal lock, now it was held together by ribbons and paste. And the bonds are getting weaker all the time.

I don't regret where I am now, I truly don't. But I have a lot of regrets about how I got here, and most of those regrets lead back to Stuart and the secrets I'd kept.

And now, because of that chain reaction I'd started, this wonderful man was no longer himself, and trying to talk to him felt like shouting across a canyon. The words went out, but nothing came back.

And if I was being really honest—brutally, painfully honest—I'd never been able to talk to him the way I could talk to Eric. Eric had always understood me—even without words. He knew the dark parts and loved me anyway.

But Eric had been dead. At least until he wasn't.

Suddenly, I had two husbands.

And the freakish truth is that I miss both of them, and I do want Stuart back.

But today, when I'd thought about my husband, it was Eric's face I saw. Not Stuart's.

And what the hell was I supposed to do about that?

Nothing.

The word filled my head, and it was right. I needed to focus on training the kids and figuring out what Stuart's prophecy means.

The ruby bleeds? I mean, come on. Prophecies always want you to do something, so why make them so damn cryptic?

"Kate."

I jumped a mile, then whipped around and threw a box of Kleenex at Eric. "What the hell? You scared me to death."

"Kleenex? This is your new approach to self-defense?"

I crossed my arms, telling myself that my pulse had kicked up because he'd startled me. Not for any other unrelated and unwanted reason. "What do you want?"

He didn't answer. Just stepped inside, closed the door behind him, and crossed to me.

"Dammit, Eric. You can't just barge in."

But that's as far as I got, because suddenly his hands were cupping my face, and his mouth was on mine and, damn me, I was melting.

The kiss was everything I remembered. Everything I'd been trying to forget. Heat and hunger and the soul-deep recognition of someone who knew exactly how to take me apart.

I wanted to melt into it. God, I wanted to. My body was already responding, leaning into him, my fingers curling into the fabric of his shirt—

I pulled back.

"Eric. No."

He didn't let go immediately. His forehead rested against mine, both of us breathing hard, the space between us charged with everything we weren't saying.

"I want to," I whispered, because maybe I owed him that. "You know I do. But I can't."

"Can't? Or won't?"

"Does it matter?"

He pulled back, just enough to look at me. His eyes were dark, unreadable. "I suppose not."

I expected anger. Frustration, at least. But he just nodded slowly, like he'd known this was coming.

"I get it," he said. "I don't like it, but I do get it." His lips curved into a small, rueful smile. "Just don't expect me to give up."

"Eric, don't."

"I know you, Kate. Better than anyone." He brushed a strand of hair from my face, the gesture achingly tender. "You made vows, and you'll keep them even when they're killing you. I get that. I respect it, even."

The smile faded and he stepped closer. "But sooner or later, you're going to have to choose. And when you do, I'll be here."

He kissed my forehead—soft, almost chaste—and turned to leave.

I forced myself not to stop him. Dug my nails into my palms and kept my mouth shut and watched him walk toward the door.

He paused.

My heart stuttered. Here it was. He was going to try again, push harder, and I wasn't sure I had the strength to say no twice.

But he wasn't looking at me. He was looking at my

dressing table. At the drawing taped to the mirror. "What is that?"

"Timmy drew it. A door. I like how he put the extra door-knob down low. I guess that's so little boys can get in, too."

He stood there for a long moment, just staring at the drawing.

"Uh, Eric? What's so fascinating about Timmy's door?"

"What? Oh. It just reminds me of something, but I can't think of what. Quite the little artist you've got there."

I laughed. "According to Fran, that's all he draws these days. Zillions of them. It's like he's Monet and doors are his water lilies."

"Weird but cute," he finally said, and I couldn't disagree.

"Sweet dreams, Katie-kins."

And then he was gone, the door clicking shut behind him, leaving me alone with the wine and the silence and the feeling that I'd just missed something important.

I looked at the drawing again. Red rectangles. Gold dots. Doors.

Just a child's drawing. Just Timmy being Timmy.

So why couldn't I shake the chill that had settled in my chest?

11

ALLIE

*S*eventeen.

I was officially seventeen years old, and Mindy had gone completely overboard, taking full advantage of Mom telling her to "have at it" when Mindy had begged to be the party planner.

"It's not overboard," she retorted after I'd said as much.

I lifted my brows. "Really?"

She shrugged, and as we followed the path toward the side garden, I let my gaze sweep over the approximately nine billion fairy lights she'd strung through every tree and along every railing.

Ahead of us, I could see the group gathered near the long table—Mom laughing at something Aunt Laura had said, Gramps holding court in one of the garden chairs, Daddy at the grill with a spatula in hand. Near the fountain, Timmy and Elena were playing some elaborate game that involved running in circles and shrieking, while Fran watched from a nearby bench, coffee cup in hand.

Signora Micari was fussing over the food table, of course,

and I breathed in the scent of her pasta sauce, one of my favorite things in the world.

"It's completely overboard," I repeated as I hip-butted my bestie. "And I totally love it."

Sophie and Ana hurried ahead of us, then grabbed chips from the bowl on the table. Stuart caught my eye and winked. I grinned back. He's not my father, but he is my dad. And considering those pre-teen and teen years he survived, maybe the visions make sense. I mean, the man's clearly a saint.

"So it's really okay?" Mindy asked.

"Are you kidding? It's freaking amazing." And it was—all the fairy lights, the incredible spread of food, the wrapped presents. There was even a HAPPY 17TH ALLIE banner strung between two oaks, the crooked letters suggesting that Timmy had helped. "I love it," I said, giving Mindy a squeeze. "Thank you."

"Don't thank me yet. Wait until you've seen the cake. It totally rocks."

She pulled me toward the far corner of the garden, where a separate table held three tiers of white frosting and delicate gold scrollwork. Seventeen candles flickered on top, already lit. And right in the middle of the top layer was the coolest cake topper I'd ever seen. "OMG! It looks just like my stiletto." It really did, too. The marzipan topper was an edible clone of the pearl-handled weapon Mom had given me on my fifteenth birthday.

Mindy shrugged. "The lady at the bakery thought it was weird. But now she has a great story about the freaky girl with a weapon for a cake topper."

"You're insane."

"I prefer *creatively committed*."

Everyone was gathering now, drifting toward the cake table. Jared caught my eye from across the garden and smiled —and I felt my heart do its usual gymnastics routine. Zane said something to make Eliza laugh, and Marcus and Cutter abandoned whatever conversation they'd been having to join the crowd.

"Make a wish!" Mindy commanded.

I closed my eyes and wished what I'd been wishing almost nightly since I learned about demons—that all of these people survive tomorrow and the next day and the next. That we figure out the freaky prophecy, and that we kick serious demon ass. Then I blew out the candles to cheers and applause.

"Speech!" Ren called out because he was a menace.

"No speeches. I will literally fight anyone who makes me give a speech."

"That's my girl," Daddy said. "Turn seventeen and immediately threaten violence."

My girl. I melted a little, because there I was standing with the people I loved, including a father who'd come back from the dead. I may have a freaky and dangerous life, but it's also seriously cool.

The moment the last note of the happy birthday song faded, Mindy swooped in with a knife and started passing out slices as the party swirled around us in comfortable chaos.

"Present time!" Mom called after everyone had cake, and I found myself in one of the comfy, cushioned yard chairs surrounded by wrapped boxes and gift bags that I dug into with gusto. Or, more specifically, Timmy did, since I let him help unwrap each gift and then play with the ribbons and bows.

"Wow," I heard myself repeating in various inflections as gift after gift was revealed. A new leather jacket from Aunt Laura. A set of throwing knives from Gramps—"Good balance, tested 'em myself." A silver bracelet from Mindy with a charm shaped like a tiny stiletto—"To match your cake." And so many more wonderful gifts.

As the pile shrank, Stuart passed me a small velvet box with a purple bow. "From me," he said.

I opened it to find a small glass vial with a crystal-and-cork stopper nestled among purple tissue paper. It had a silver band around the neck, which connected the vial to a delicate silver chain. Beneath the necklace, I found a photograph—Stuart and me on the beach, arms around each other, both of us laughing at something I couldn't remember anymore.

"It's holy water," he said as I blinked back silly, sentimental tears. "The vial's been in my family for generations. I had a jeweler put a collar on it so you could wear it." He shrugged, suddenly awkward. "I want to help keep you as safe as possible, kiddo."

My throat went tight. "Stuart..."

I hugged him hard, blinking back tears, and noticed that Mom was wiping away tears of her own.

I sniffled as we broke apart, looking away to hide the embarrassment of a teenager hugging their dad. As I did, it clicked that Mom wasn't standing beside him. There'd been weirdness between them ever since Stuart woke from the coma, and I couldn't help but remember the time I burst in on Mom and Daddy doing a lot more than she'd caught me and Jared doing.

And then I couldn't help but wonder if—even though he'd been in a coma at the time—Stuart somehow knew about that.

Because, if so...whoa. Major awkward.

With a mental *oomph*, I shoved the memory aside, because *so* not wanting to cringe again. But at the same time, I was hopeful. I wanted Mom and Daddy back together. I really did. But that would mean Mom and Stuart weren't, and I didn't want to think about Stuart getting hurt.

I sighed. If this was adulting, it kind of sucked.

But, since I wasn't yet an adult according to the State of

California, I tossed all those confusing thoughts aside, then wiggled my fingers and said, "Next! Gimme, gimme."

"This one's from your father and me," Mom said as Daddy handed me a pink-wrapped box then moved back to stand beside Mom, the sentimental look that passed between them making my chest tighten all over again. I ripped off the paper with a flourish and opened the box. Inside, nestled in velvet, was a stunning crossbow. Compact, elegant, clearly old but perfectly maintained. The wood was dark and polished, the metalwork intricate and beautiful. "Wow."

"I gave it to your father when we were active in *Forza*," Mom said. Her voice was rough, and I knew she was holding back *my baby's growing-up* tears.

"It's yours, sweetheart," Daddy said. "You've earned it."

I lifted it carefully, feeling the weight, the balance. Perfect. Like it had been made for my hands.

"I don't know what to say. I mean, thank you, but...wow."

Stuart's phone buzzed, and as he glanced at the screen, his expression shifted to something I couldn't read. "I need to take this, kiddo," he said. "It's Rome."

I nodded, then watched him disappear through the French doors, his phone pressed to his ear. And I couldn't help but think that he was probably glad of the distraction, what with Mom and Daddy strolling down Memory Lane.

Jared appeared beside me as everyone started to drift back toward the food and conversation. "Hey," he said, his voice low. "Can I steal you for a second?"

I set the crossbow carefully back in its box and let him lead me toward the edge of the garden, away from the crowd. My heart did that fluttery thing it always did when he looked at me like that—like I was the only person in the world.

"I wanted to give you this in private," he said, handing me a tiny package wrapped in red paper. I opened it carefully to reveal a typical department store jewelry box. I grinned up at

Jared, expecting to find a bracelet or some other piece of jewelry he'd seen me admire.

Instead, I found a treasure. A ring of delicate silver filigree cradling a small blue stone that caught the fairy lights and scattered them like tiny stars.

"It was my mother's," he said, slipping it on my right forefinger, the only finger it fit. "She always meant for it to go to Celia." He shrugged. "I never gave it to her. I'm not sure why. Once we were turned, and she was going to be ten forever, it just seemed like a reminder of what she'd never have. But I've always loved the ring. And now I think maybe it was somehow always really meant for you."

I blinked back tears, thinking of sweet Celia. I missed her, too. I can only imagine how much Jared's heart still hurt. "No," I whispered. "It was always meant for her. And that makes you giving it to me even more special."

His smile was tremulous as he brushed away the tear that snaked down my cheek. "I love you, Alison Elizabeth Crowe," he whispered.

"I know, I whispered back. I love you, too." He pulled me to him, and his soft moan seemed to echo through me. It was the first time we'd said it out loud. But we both knew. We'd both known for a long time.

"It's not an engagement ring," he added quickly. "I don't need your mom staking me."

"Chicken."

"Happy birthday," he said again, and for a moment, standing there in the fairy lights with Jared's ring on my finger and his hand in mine, everything felt absolutely right.

Then the side gate exploded inward and shot all of that to hell

12

ALLIE

*W*ood splintered and metal screeched and then they were pouring through, fast and wrong, and hungry.

Demons—a lot of them.

"Get Timmy and Elena inside!" Mom shouted, already moving, a stiletto appearing in her hand like magic.

Fran scooped up Elena, but Timmy was on the other side of the garden, frozen in place, his eyes huge.

"Timster!" I called, moving that direction. But Trevor was already sprinting that way, and without slowing down, he grabbed Timmy around the waist, and bolted inside as a broad-shouldered demon lunged, pinning me down. He smiled as he straddled me, and it was the smile of something that had been waiting a long time. "Pretty girlie gonna die."

I didn't like the sound of that. I also didn't like the fact that I'd been stupid enough to put my weapons down during present time. Not that the lack of a weapon slowed me down —it didn't. It just meant my defense option sucked.

I did it anyway, cringing as I shoved my finger into his eye —all the way up to Celia's ring—and then I sighed with satisfaction as I saw the telltale shimmer that indicated the demon had left the building.

I shoved his fallen body off me, then bolted to the table where I'd left my stiletto. I wanted the crossbow, but now was not the time to get familiar with a new weapon.

A quick glance around and I found Jared as he sped over the grass to tear into a hunchbacked demon that he'd been advancing on Aunt Laura. One twist, one strike, and the demon dropped.

Mom and Cutter were both on the slope that led down to the cemetery, each fighting a demon of their own, and working in perfect sync. I looked around for Stuart, then remembered he'd gone inside for a phone call. I hoped desperately that he was safe in there, along with Signora Micari and the kids.

As for the others, Marcus was holding his own and Gramps was making a meal of the demon who probably thought it would have it easy attacking an old man.

I looked for Zane but didn't see him, and I said a silent prayer that he was safe inside. I was about to go check the mansion to make sure no demon had breached it, but I stopped cold.

Sophie.

She was facing a demon alone—a woman in a designer business suit trying to tear Sophie's throat out. Sophie was backing up, one of the cake forks shaking in her hand, and I started to run toward her—

But I didn't need to.

She feinted left, and when the demon lunged, she drove her fork straight through its eye. The body dropped. Sophie stood there, breathing hard, looking a bit queasy as she stared at what she'd done.

"Holy shit," she finally whispered.

"Good kill!" I shouted, and she looked up at me with an expression that was equal parts terror and triumph.

Then I heard Daddy's cry of pure, deep pain, and my blood went cold.

He was on the ground, his shirt ripped open and his chest bleeding as he struggled to stand straight—to protect Trevor, who was pressed against the garden wall, his eyes wide with horror.

I knew in an instant what had happened—Trevor had taken Timmy inside, then returned to help, only to land in a demon's crosshairs. Daddy had taken the hit for him, but he'd only bought a few minutes, and now a true demon loomed over them both. Not the kind of demon we usually encounter, all tucked nicely into a human shell.

No, this demon was showing its actual form, something they very rarely did because a demon killed in its true form was really dead and done. A demon inhabiting a dead human just zipped back to the ether to wait another turn.

This one was real all right. Claws and fangs and scales and everything that horror movies had gotten right over the years, plus a lot more. And that monster was bearing down on my dad with claws and teeth, already having drawn blood.

Too much blood.

"No!" The word ripped out of me, and I was running toward Daddy, but Zane got there first.

He slammed into the demon from the side, and they both went down, rolling and grappling on the packed ground until Zane's blade found its mark. But not before the demon's claws raked across his chest, leaving bloody furrows in their wake.

I rushed forward as Zane staggered to his feet, one hand pressed to his chest, blood seeping between his fingers.

And then it was over.

Eight demons. All dead. The garden was wrecked—tables

overturned, fairy lights tangled and broken, the birthday banner hanging by one corner.

I ran to Daddy, breathing in the sulphur-scented musk left behind by our attackers.

"I'm okay," he said, but his voice was strained, and his face was gray. "It's not as bad as it looks."

Mom got there on my heels, and she pressed her hand against the wounds.

That's when I saw it. Something I'd never seen in my mom's eyes before. Fear. Real, bone-deep terror.

"Don't move," she said, and her voice cracked. "Marcus! I need you!"

Marcus appeared with a med kit. "Let me see," he said, gently moving Mom's hands. He examined the wound, then nodded. "It's deep, but clean. Missed anything vital. He'll need stitches, but he'll be fine."

Mom let out a breath that sounded like it had been trapped in her chest for years.

Jared was at my side suddenly, his hand on my shoulder. "You okay?"

I nodded, not trusting my voice. His shirt was torn, and there was blood on his hands—demon blood, not his.

I looked around the garden. Sophie was sitting on the ground, staring at her bloody hands. Zane was letting Eliza press a cloth to his chest wound, his jaw tight with pain. Trevor hadn't moved from the wall—he was still shaking, tears streaming down his face.

Gramps limped over to stand next to me. "Eight demons," he said, his voice grim. "A coordinated attack on our students. That's not random."

"No," I agreed. "It's not."

"It's all connected," I said quietly. "Antonio. The prophecy. This attack. It's all to do with the same thing."

Gramps nodded grimly. "Can't argue with that. Now tell me why."

I shook my head. "I don't know."

He grunted. "Well, that's the name of the game, isn't it, kiddo? We figure it out, or we die trying."

"I'm not sure I like that game, I said.

Eddie snorted. "Then you signed up for the wrong gig."

"Like I signed up." Except I did. Even before knowing what I was, I'd wanted in. And even now, I didn't want out. Instead, I wanted answers. And pay back.

Right then, though, I just felt drained, and I leaned against Jared. He had no heat to keep me warm, but I didn't need heat. I just needed him. And answers.

As we all headed back inside, I turned briefly to look at the wreckage of my seventeenth birthday party—the smashed cake, the scattered presents, the splattered blood.

But we'd won.

Happy birthday to me.

13

ALLIE

"Movie after training?" Jared asked as we took the stairs from the second-floor balcony down to the school's backyard and the huge cemetery it abuts. Ancient and spooky, which makes it a great training area with the kind of demony vibe that gets you in a kick-ass frame of mind.

At the moment, I hoped Jared's mind was elsewhere.

"Movie?"

He shrugged. "I saw they added some new stuff to the streaming queue."

"Depends on what you're thinking." I shot him a sideways look. "If you say horror, I'm vetoing."

"Good," he said, "because I've had enough demons and training and practice battles over the last few days."

I was right there with him. The last five days after the demons attacked the party had been crazy, with Mom and Daddy and Marcus and Cutter going into major overdrive on training, and dragging me along with them to teach, demonstrate, spar, whatever.

And, yes, it made a difference—the newbies were doing

great, and they all have a new level of confidence—but at this point, I was actually craving an assignment that required opening a musty old book and tracing a demon's lineage.

"Not action or horror," Jared assured me. "Honestly, I was thinking we could pick something with less plot and more...atmosphere."

"Atmosphere," I repeated as my cheeks warmed. "Is that what we're calling it now?"

His grin was slow and deliberate. "I have no idea what you're implying."

"Uh-huh."

He flashed me the sexy grin that always makes me melt, then held my hand as we paused on the stairs with the grounds spread out in front of us. The sloping lawn, the old stone path, and beyond that, the cemetery where my parents had found Antonio's body at the start of the semester.

The side gate from my literal party crashers had been repaired, but I could still see the pile of lumber that Stuart and Ren had used to fix it.

The sun had set over an hour ago, and the moon was rising, painting everything in a silvery glow. For a moment, it almost looked peaceful. Like a normal school with normal students and normal problems.

We reached the bottom of the stairs and saw Eliza and Sophie waving from a few yards down the path.

"Hey," Sophie said with her sweet smile that we'd only newly discovered. Over the last few days, she'd been coming out of her shell—and doing great in training. Part of that's probably because of Eliza's steady mentoring, but most is because she kicked ass on my birthday. And that kind of ass-kicking is a serious confidence builder.

Trust me. I know these things.

"Hey," Eliza said. "Heading out?"

"Just a walk." I gestured vaguely toward the cemetery. "Needed some air."

"Watch where you wander," Eliza said, her tone teasing. "Zane went down there a while ago. Said he wanted to clear his head. We wouldn't want anyone to interrupt any…private moments."

"Eliza!" Sophie practically squeaked the word, and I shot Eliza a scowl. She definitely wasn't following the Approved Kate Connor Rules of Mentoring.

"We'll be careful," Jared said dryly. "Wouldn't want to traumatize the new kid."

"Too late," Eliza said. "Pretty sure watching you two spar yesterday already did that."

"That wasn't sparring," Jared said with a glance toward me. "That was me losing badly."

I shrugged. "You're the one who said not to pull my punches. Don't say it if you don't mean it."

He tapped my nose. "I love you."

"So you've said," I teased as my cheeks went pink. Saying it that first time had opened a dam, and we said it to each other all the time now.

This, however, was a first—saying it in front of other people. Or, more specifically, saying it to each other in front of other people, without having first told my mom our new status quo. That, I think, is what qualifies as a major mom/daughter fail.

With a small grimace, Jared turned to Eliza and Sophie, who were both blushing as hard as I was. "So, yeah. Maybe don't mention to Kate that I said that. I'd rather not be staked in my sleep. Or to Eric, for that matter. Or Stuart."

He paused, then shrugged. "Not Eddie, either. Actually, you know what? Just don't mention it to anyone."

Eliza was trying so hard not to laugh that she looked like she had to pee.

"We won't mention it," Sophie said. "We don't have to. Everyone already knows."

She wasn't wrong.

"Come on, Soph," Eliza said, still giggling. "Let's do some weights, then stream *Rocky.*"

Once they were back inside, we continued down the hillside toward the cemetery, our fingers twined. "Come on," he said, tugging my hand as we reached the flat ground of the cemetery, stretching out around us.

Some people think cemeteries are creepy, but I loved this place. It had a quiet, settled feeling. Not creepy. Just...patient. Like it had seen a lot and wasn't surprised by much anymore.

And—bonus points—when we'd first started to fix up the mansion to become the school, Daddy and I had made a powder from the bones of saints, then spread it over the ground. And presto—demon and zombie deterrence courtesy of actual saint remains provided by the Vatican.

And an idea I'm still pretty proud of.

"So," I said, because comfortable silences were nice, but I wanted to hear his voice. "The attack. You still haven't told me what you thought of how the students did."

"Sure, I did," he said. "I told you that night." He pitched his voice low as he continued. "You just forgot because you had other things on your mind."

"By now, you should know better than to tell me anything important when we're cuddling."

He chuckled. "Fair. And same goes. As for the kids—"

"Students," I corrected.

"Trevor's the one who really surprised me," he said. "The way he got Timmy to safety—no hesitation. And then he came back out. Kid could've stayed inside where it was safe, but he soldiered on."

"And almost got himself killed for it."

"But he didn't. Your dad made sure of that." Jared paused. "How's Eric doing, by the way?"

"Good. Marcus says the stitches can come out in a few more days. Mom's been hovering, which is driving him crazy." I kicked at a loose stone. "He keeps saying he's fine, but I saw those wounds. That demon would've torn Trevor apart."

"Your dad's tough. And now Trevor owes him."

"Daddy doesn't see it like that. We're all in this together. No one owes anybody anything."

Jared shrugged. "True. But even so, isn't paying back a mortal debt the karmically polite thing to do?"

"Maybe. I guess so. I mean, I would. So would you, right?"

"I would," Jared said. "But I don't think Trevor sees it that way. I think he's more in your dad's camp."

"Really? Did he say something?"

"Nothing like that. He's been even more withdrawn since the attack. Like he's embarrassed that he needed saving. I could be wrong, but I've met a lot of folks over the last hundred-plus years. You get a sense."

"That's fair," I said. "But maybe he's not embarrassed. Maybe he's grateful and doesn't know how to show it."

"Could be." Jared shrugged. "I've known plenty of people who hid their better qualities behind bad attitudes. Sometimes it's the only armor they have."

I thought about that. Trevor had barely spoken to anyone since arriving, and when he did, it was usually something sharp or dismissive. But Jared was right—when it mattered, he'd moved without thinking. Saved Timmy. Came back to help. That meant something.

"What about Zane?" I asked.

Jared didn't answer right away. We'd reached the edge of the cemetery now, and he paused, looking out over the rows of weathered headstones.

"He's good," Jared finally said. "Really good. Taking down

that true-form demon—that's not easy. Most hunters never even see one."

"He got hurt doing it."

"He did. And he didn't hesitate. The guy's got guts." Jared's brow furrowed slightly. "But..."

"But what?"

He shrugged, a gesture that managed to convey frustration. "I don't know. Something about him rubs me the wrong way. Can't put my finger on it."

I studied his profile. Jared had seen things, survived things, and developed those spooky vampire instincts. If something was pinging his radar about Zane...

Then again, Zane had been nothing but helpful since arriving. Friendly, skilled, good with the other students. He'd literally taken claws across his chest to save my dad.

"He does seem to avoid you," I said slowly, remembering a couple of times when Jared had sat near Zane in the common area...and Zane had suddenly remembered he needed something from his dorm room. "Have you noticed? Like, he's fine with everyone else, but whenever you're around, he finds somewhere else to be."

"I noticed."

"Maybe he's just weirded out. You know—the vampire thing."

Jared made a noncommittal sound. "Maybe."

"Give him time. He's new, he's adjusting, and you can be a little intimidating."

He cocked his head. "I'm not intimidating."

"Oh, please. You're a hundred and twenty-seven years old and you drink blood. That's at least a little intimidating." To be fair, Jared didn't drink human blood—that stuff was like a drug to vamps. He stuck to the animal kind. But since Jared had yet to give the *Intro to Vampires* lecture yet, the newbies' only point of reference was pop culture.

"Fair point," he conceded as we wandered deeper into the cemetery, past the older graves with their crumbling angels and worn inscriptions, toward the newer section where the headstones were simpler but better maintained. I didn't see Zane anywhere—he'd probably already headed back, and that was just fine with me. I wanted this time with Jared. Just the two of us, away from the chaos of the school.

"Here," Jared said, stopping near a low stone bench tucked between two ancient oaks. "This is a good spot."

I sat down, and he settled beside me, close enough that our shoulders touched. Above us, the first stars were beginning to emerge, faint pinpricks against the darkening sky.

"Remember when you first showed me the stars?"

"I remember you couldn't name a single constellation."

"I still can't. That's what I have you for."

He pointed upward. "That's Orion. The three stars in a row are his belt."

"Okay, I do know that one. But everyone knows that one."

"Fine. That cluster there—see it? That's the Pleiades. The Seven Sisters."

I squinted. "I see like...four stars."

"Your mortal eyes are failing you."

"Rude."

He laughed softly, and I leaned into him, letting my head rest against his shoulder. The night was cool but not cold, and his body was solid and familiar beside me. This was what I needed. Not demon hunting or prophecies or trying to figure out why eight demons had attacked my birthday party. Just this. Just us.

"Do you ever think about what it'll be like?" I asked quietly. "Years from now, I mean. When I'm older, and you're...not."

His arm came around me, pulling me closer. "Sometimes."

"Does it scare you?"

"Yes." The word was simple. Honest. "But not enough to make me walk away."

"Even though I'll get old? Gray hair, wrinkles, the whole thing?"

"Even then." He pressed a kiss to the top of my head. "You'll always be beautiful to me, Allie. At seventeen or sixty or a hundred and six."

"I probably won't make it to ninety-six, much less a hundred and six. Most humans don't. And demon hunting isn't exactly a longevity-friendly profession."

"Then I'll enjoy every moment I have with you." His voice was steady, but I could hear the edge beneath it—the fear he usually kept buried. Because let's face it, my job was definitely a hardhat kind of gig. Only I was never issued a hardhat.

I tilted my head up to look at him, this immortal being who looked as fragile as the rest of us.

Human. He looked it because that's what he used to be, and it was sometimes easy to forget that he'd shed his human cloak a long, long time ago.

"I love you," I said. "You know that, right? That it's true, and not just pretty words?"

"I know." He kissed me then, soft and slow, and I let myself sink into it. Let myself forget, just for a moment, about everything waiting for us back at the school.

When we finally pulled apart, the stars had fully emerged, scattered across the sky like diamonds on black velvet. I curled against his side, his arm still around me, and we sat there in the quiet cemetery, watching the universe turn overhead.

"So about that movie," I said eventually. "The one with...atmosphere."

I felt him smile against my hair. "Still interested?"

"Maybe." I traced a pattern on his chest, feeling his stillness beneath my fingers. No heartbeat. No breath. Just Jared, steady and eternal. "We should probably head back before they send a search party."

"Probably." He didn't move.

Neither did I.

The movie could wait. Everything could wait. Right now, I just wanted to stay there, suspended between the earth and the stars, pretending that the world wasn't about to fall apart around us.

It wouldn't last. Nothing ever did.

But for now—for this one quiet moment—it was enough.

He squeezed my hand, and we started walking back toward the mansion.

We'd made it maybe halfway up the path when I spotted him—a figure sitting on one of the old stone benches near the cemetery gate, head tilted back, looking up at the sky.

Zane.

"Hey," I called out as we approached. "Eliza said you were down here."

He turned, and for just a second—so fast I almost missed it—something like irritation flickered across his face. Then the easy smile slid into place, and he waved us over.

"Couldn't sleep," he said. "Figured I'd get some air."

"Still thinking about the attack?" I asked.

Zane grimaced. "Is that weird? It's been days, but I can't get it out of my head. Seeing that true demon." He shuddered. "I mean, I feel pretty damn powerless against something like that. Like it's there all the time, right there with me. Hidden and just waiting to pounce."

"That's the way of demons. And it's not weird at all to be thinking about it. But you need to focus on the positive. We got through it, remember?"

"She's right," Jared said. "It would be weird if you weren't still thinking about it. For one thing, you're new to this life.

For another, eight damn demons? They're not creatures that usually hunt in packs."

"Seriously scary packs," Zane said. "I mean, I watch TV, . but that was beyond." He shrugged. "But I guess that's going to be my new normal."

"It doesn't have to be," I said. "We found you because you fit a profile, but you can opt out."

He shrugged, then shook his head. "Honestly, I don't think I can." He paused for a bit, then rushed on. "I mean, now that I know. Hard to walk away when you know what's hiding in the dark."

"I'm glad to hear it," I said truthfully. And then, because he was finally opening up, I decided to forego a bit of alone time with Jared. "I think you'll be an asset."

"Thanks." He stood, brushing off his jeans. "How's your dad doing?"

"Better."

"Glad to hear it." He started moving past us. "I'll get out of your way," he said with a glance between Jared and me that looked a little like a leer, though I was probably making that up. Residual embarrassment stemming from where I hoped this walk with Jared would lead.

I started to tell him he could stay, but he was leaving to give us privacy, and, honestly, that sounded pretty good to me.

"I'm just not sure of him," Jared said quietly after Zane disappeared up the stone steps toward the mansion.

"Really? Why?"

Jared shrugged. "Can't put my finger on it."

I laughed. "Must be a guy thing. I'm pretty sure Sophie and Ana and Mindy are all half in love with him. Oh, and Signora. She always gives him a bigger portion."

"But not you?"

I met his grin with one of my own, then hooked my arm through his. "I remain immune."

He laughed, and we were about to start walking again when I noticed the small pile of dirt beside the bench. "Maybe he was smoking," Jared suggested. "Made himself an emergency ashtray."

I cringed. "Mom's going to have a cow. Hunters don't smoke. Reduces breath capacity.

"Well, don't say anything to her yet. No point getting her worked up if it turns out a family of moles has moved in."

"True enough," I said, though the idea of a mole infestation didn't make me happy. I loved the colorful flower beds that surrounded the mansion. And, yes, a horde of demons had already destroyed the side garden, but demons I could fight. Moles, though? That sounded like a landscaping nightmare.

And I had enough nightmares to juggle already, thank you very much.

14

KATE

"I've found something."

I blinked at Marcus, trying to make sense of those words as I warmed my hands on my coffee mug. Unless a demon forces the issue—or Timmy—I don't wake up well. Which was why I was hiding in the kitchen pretending to review training schedules while nursing my third cup of coffee and staring blankly at a spreadsheet that might as well have been written in Aramaic.

Now, however, my brain cells started to fire. "Something about Antonio?"

Mindy had managed to hack the USB drive's password a few days ago, and Marcus had been printing out documents and poring over paper ever since. I'd checked in on him twice, found him surrounded by stacks of printouts covered in his cramped handwriting, and quietly backed away. Marcus doesn't usually do research, but since this is about Antonio, he was going all in, and I knew that doing the research was his way of working through his grief.

"Come with me," he said, which wasn't an answer at all.

I wasn't about to argue, though, so me and my coffee

followed Marcus through the mansion's quiet hallways. Morning light filtered through the tall windows, casting long rectangles of gold across the hardwood floors. From the dorm area wing, I could hear the muffled sounds of students moving around—footsteps, a door closing, someone laughing. Normal sounds of a school going about its morning business.

We passed the sitting room where Laura was huddled with Stuart, both of them bent over laptops, probably reviewing the budget or some other essential administrative thing I was grateful not to have to think about. Stuart looked up as we passed, and something in his expression made me pause—that distant look he got far too frequently now, like he was seeing something the rest of us couldn't. But then he blinked, and it was gone, and he went back to his computer.

I made a mental note to check on him later, then followed Marcus into the library. Thanks to Eric's love of rare books and his training as both a Hunter and an *alimentatore*—essentially a research guru—the school's library is a bibliophile's dream. Floor-to-ceiling shelves crammed with ancient texts, leather spines cracked and faded with age. Research tables scattered with papers and artifacts. The smell of old books and older secrets.

Usually, I loved this room. But it wasn't a place that Marcus frequently visited as a combat trainer, and when he made a point of closing the door behind us, I shivered as an invisible cloak of dread seemed to settle over me.

When we reached the biggest table in the center of the room, I saw why we were here—Marcus had spread Antonio's materials across its surface like evidence at a crime scene. Which, I supposed, it was. Printouts. Photographs. Photocopies of documents so old the text was barely legible.

"Thank God for Mindy," Marcus said, closing the heavy doors behind him. "That kid's a whiz at research."

"So what do we have?" I asked, glancing at the closed

doors. This was bad. This was something he didn't want anyone else to hear about. Not yet.

"A lot. Maybe some answers." He paused, his expression strained as he added, "A few things you won't want to see."

I drew in a breath. "Whatever it is, just tell me. I'm sure I've dealt with worse." I expected a snarky comment in response.

I didn't get one.

Instead, Marcus selected a printout from the pile and slid it toward me. The text was in Latin—because of course it was —but certain words jumped out at me even with my rusty translation skills. *Sanguinis*. Blood. *Porta*. Door. *Terra sacra*, consecrated earth. There was also a word I didn't recognize, repeated throughout the document like a heartbeat— Samarek. A name, I assumed. And considering who I was and what I did, I assumed it was the name of a demon.

"What am I looking at?"

He pulled out a chair and sat, then gestured for me to do the same. "Antonio was researching a ritual. Something called Samarek's Rite. It's old—medieval, maybe older. References to it appear in texts the Vatican has kept locked away for centuries. Forbidden knowledge, even by Forza standards."

"Samarek," I said. "I haven't heard of him."

"Old. Doesn't slide into our world often. And when he does, it's usually bad." He pulled another document from the pile—this one a photo of a page from an illuminated manuscript, the margins decorated with images that made my skin crawl. Twisted figures. Writhing shapes. And in the center, something that might have been human once, if you squinted and ignored the horrific wrongness of its proportions.

"According to Antonio's research, Samarek started out human. But ages ago, he began trading pieces of his humanity for demonic power."

I shuddered as I studied the illustration of the thing that had once been a man. "Trading how?" I asked, keeping my voice level when I really wanted to cringe and

say, "Eww."

"Literally how? No idea. But the bottom line is that he gave up a piece of himself—soul and body—and his sire demon replaced that offering with something from the other side. Over and over until there was nothing human left. Just...this," he said, tapping the illustration. "A patchwork demon, the old Hunters called him. Part human memory, part demonic corruption, all of it stitched together into something that shouldn't exist."

The coffee churned in my stomach. I'd fought a lot of demons over the years. Killed more than I could count. But this? This may well have been the creepiest thing I'd heard of.

"That's..." I couldn't find the right word. Horrifying really didn't sum up the freak factor. "Why would anyone do that?"

"Power. Immortality. The usual temptations." Marcus shrugged, but his eyes were grim. "The texts say Samarek was ambitious even as a human. A sorcerer, a scholar of dark things. He didn't want to just summon demons—he wanted to become one. To transcend human limitations entirely."

"Just when you think you've seen everything in this job..."

"Ah, but wait. It gets worse." Marcus pulled out a printout of a photograph—grainy, dark, clearly taken with a flash in poor lighting conditions. But I recognized the image immediately.

The *Signum Fidelis*. The symbol we'd found burned into Antonio's palm.

"This is Samarek's *Signum Fidelis*," Marcus said quietly. "His personal mark. Antonio had been tracking references to it for months before he died. That's why he was coming here early, breaking protocol. He found something that scared him enough to risk everything."

"Wait—he was coming here to get our help or because he thought we needed help?" Fear cut through me as I thought of Eric and Allie. Surely this freakish demon didn't consider them brethren because they had demon essence woven through their humanity.

Did he?

"Marcus?" I pressed as silence lingered. "Tell me."

He sighed, then nodded. "Okay. Okay, here's the thing. The ritual I mentioned earlier—Samarek's Rite—it's blood magic. Very dark. Very dangerous. It can channel Samarek's power for specific purposes. Healing wounds that should be fatal. Curing poisons that have no antidote. Saving lives that should be lost."

"But there's a price," I said, because there was always a price.

He nodded, then pulled one more document from the pile —I recognized it right away. One of Forza's log sheets, part of an internal file that had kept track of hunter activities for millennia.

"Antonio found this in the archives. It's a report from over twenty years ago. A hunter named Gregory Mathes performed Samarek's Rite in Rome."

Gregory Mathes. The name tugged at something in my memory. "Oh," I finally said. "We worked with him a few times, back when Eric and I were still in Rome. Older guy. He'd been like a mentor to Eric for a while. You're telling me he performed the Rite?"

Marcus nodded. "He performed the ritual to save someone who was dying. Someone who'd been poisoned by demonic venom and had only minutes to live."

I went completely cold, my heart pounding in my ears.

I didn't want to look at that document. Didn't want to see what I already knew was written there.

"The ritual required blood," Marcus continued, his voice soft. "Specific blood. From someone whose soul was connected to the dying person. Someone who loved them."

"Marcus, no."

He met my eyes, and I saw the sympathy there. The sorrow. "Eric's name is on that report. He was the blood donor. And the person Gregory saved…"

He didn't finish the sentence. He didn't have to.

I looked down at the document. Read the words I'd been dreading. Eric's blood. A demon's bargain.

And my life saved.

But at what price?

15

KATE

I found him in the training room.

The space was large and open, designed for combat practice—padded floors, mirrored walls, racks of weapons along one side. Eric stood in the center, working through forms with his blade. The movements were precise, economical, the kind of muscle memory that only came from decades of practice. Thrust. Parry. Spin. Strike.

He was beautiful when he fought. I'd always thought so. Even now, with my heart hammering and my hands shaking and twenty years of secrets—again—sitting like poison in my gut, he still called to me, this man I could watch for eternity.

He turned when I came closer. And I watched the light in his eyes dim as he understood.

"Marcus put it together."

I nodded. "Did you expect less of him?"

"Never."

"Funny," I said. "I expected more of you."

"Kate."

"You and demons and the damn secrets you share," I snapped. "When is it going to stop? First, the whole demon-bound-inside-you thing that, oh, impacted our daughter's entire existence. And now I learn that you used a demonic blood ritual to cure me? That I have some of that essence, too? And you never once thought I might like to be clued in?"

He dragged his fingers through his hair. "I know. Believe me, I know. I should have told you. I did tell Father Donnelly. He said it wouldn't—well, that it wouldn't mark you permanently. That its power would be drained away by the healing."

I crossed my arms. "Great. You got off easy. What if that hadn't been the case?"

"Dammit, Kate, you were dying. I'd do the same thing again today. And you know what? I think you would, too. For Allie. For Timmy. For Stuart." He drew in a breath. "Maybe even for me."

I blinked back tears. "Fine," I snapped. "I get it. But it scares me."

He took my hands in his. "I know," he said softly. "It scared me, too. But losing you scared me more. And it wasn't like I could ask your permission. You weren't conscious. You were dying. And I would have sold my soul to save you." He drew in a breath. "I didn't have to, though. The price was only blood."

"You and I both know it's never *only* blood."

He shrugged. "You were dying. Even my life wouldn't have been too great a price."

I pulled my hands back, firm but still gentle. Because, yeah, I got that.

"You should have told me when we found Antonio," I said, but there was no bite left in my voice. "You should have told me you recognized the mark when we were in the cemetery."

"I didn't. I swear. I knew it was a *Signum Fidelis*. But I didn't know whose. Not until today when Marcus told me he'd identified the mark."

"But you suspected."

He shook his head. "No. I didn't. Honestly, Kate, why would I? That was two decades ago. With everything that's happened since then, why would seeing Antonio with a mark make me think of that horrible night and my goddamn deal with the devil to keep you alive? Katie, please. Believe me."

"I do," I said truthfully. "But Eric—*Allie*. You say it didn't impact you, but what if it did her? What if now she's connected to Samarek in some horrible way? Not just the essence of a demon, but some actual bit of that one inside her because you put its blood in me?"

A flicker of my own horror crashed over his face. "No. No. I just told you. The blood burned away with the healing. No traces left in you at all.

I studied his face, saw the certainty there. "You're sure?"

"Father Corletti would have told me if that was a risk. And he would have said something when you were pregnant. We both know that. He's not like Father Donnelly."

I hugged myself. Father Donnelly was the priest behind the whole demon-in-Eric plan to make an uber-Hunter. But he hadn't bothered to inform anyone in, oh, the Vatican until very late in the game. He's also on a branch of my family tree, a little factoid I am always trying hard to forget.

Eric reached out and tentatively took my hands. "She's fine," he said gently.

I looked down at our twined fingers. "You have to stop hiding things from me."

"No," he said, "I don't."

"Dammit, Eric," I began, but he stopped me with a finger to my lips.

"I have to tell you what affects you and Allie, but you're not my wife. Not anymore. I know because you keep reminding me."

He stroked my cheek, and despite everything, I melted a

little. "I didn't perform the ritual," he said. "I was freaked out of my mind. You had maybe minutes to live. Gregory performed the rites. I was just...the ingredient."

"The ingredient?"

"The blood source. The connection." He crossed to the bench against the wall and sank down onto it as if exhaustion had overcome him. "Mathes knew things most hunters never learn—rituals and texts the Vatican kept locked away. You remember, right?"

At my nod, he continued. "I thought I could trust him with anything, and I was beyond glad that he'd come hunting with us that night."

"What did happen that night?" I asked. "I don't remember any of it."

He hesitated, as if he didn't want to go back. I was beginning to think I'd have to push when he began, his voice low and flat. "The three of us were hunting in Trastevere," he began, referring to a historic neighborhood in Rome with a lively nightlife. "You took a hit meant for me. The demon's claws were poisoned—something ancient, something we'd never seen, and it was spreading fast. There was nothing I could do, so I picked you up and was going to try to race back to Forza."

I remembered. Fragments of it, anyway. The pain that had felt like fire spreading through my veins. The cold that had come after, numbing and final. Eric's face above me, terrified, his voice breaking as he begged me to hold on.

"Gregory said he knew a way," Eric continued. "A ritual that could channel enough power to purge the poison and heal the wounds. He said he'd read about it years ago." His voice cracked slightly as he continued. "I didn't ask questions. I didn't care about the cost. I just wanted you to live."

"What did he do?"

"He punched out the window of a closed shop, and we

went inside, then down to the basement. He cut my palm, then drew symbols on the floor in my blood. Spoke words I didn't understand—old words, in a language I'd never heard."

I shuddered. Eric's a genius with languages, ancient and modern. Even back then, if he hadn't been familiar with the language, it must have been truly rare.

Eric's hands had curled into fists on his knees. "There was a moment—just a moment—when I felt something reach through. Something vast and dark and hungry twisting inside."

A chill ran down my spine. "Samarek."

"I didn't know his name then. I just knew it was wrong. Powerful and wrong, and for a moment I was certain I'd screwed up." Pain colored his face, but then he took a breath, and his shoulders sagged as if he was reliving his relief all over again. "Then you gasped, and your eyes flew open, and the poison was gone. Just like that. Like it had never existed." He pressed the heels of his hands against his eyes, and I knew he was battling tears. I couldn't blame him. My eyes were welling, too.

"And Mathes?"

The silence stretched. Then Eric whispered, "He collapsed. Right there on the floor, next to the symbols he'd drawn. Dead before I could even try to help him."

He looked up at me, and his eyes were haunted. "That was the price, Kate. A life for a life. Gregory Mathes knew it going in. Knew someone had to pay. He chose to pay it himself so I wouldn't have to."

I stood there, trying to process. Twenty years. Twenty years of marriage and divorce and death and resurrection, and I'd never known. Never suspected that the life I was living— every breath, every moment—had been bought with another man's sacrifice.

"So the ritual closed when Gregory died. That was the exchange."

"Yes. Whatever door he'd opened, whatever connection he'd made to Samarek's power—it sealed when his heart stopped." Eric's jaw tightened.

"If you'd asked—if Gregory had told you the ceremony would kill him—would you have done it anyway?"

He didn't hesitate. "If he were truly offering? Yes. To save you, I would have said yes in a heartbeat."

I blinked, fighting tears. "And what about now? I mean, why is he back? Why come here? Why kill Antonio?"

"I've been thinking about that since Marcus told me it was Samarek's mark. I don't know." He drew in a stuttering breath. "But I have a guess."

I felt suddenly cold. Eric's guesses were as good as gold. And I could already tell that this one scared him.

"What? Dammit, Eric, what?"

"The Gate."

It took me a second to figure out where he was going with that. When I did, I gasped.

"Allie," I whispered. "You think he's here for Allie?"

"She closed the gate," he said. And that she had.

Our daughter had prevented the freaking apocalypse by closing and locking a gate to hell that was about to burst open and would have released a massive number of theretofore trapped demons.

A side benefit was that the gate she'd shut was connected to other gates all through our realm of existence, each connected to the other by a spiderweb of demony mystical threads. To be honest, I don't fully understand how it works —that's Eric's thing. But I do understand the end result. Smaller gates all over the planet closed and locked that day, too.

And if one of those gates was Samarek's back door, then my daughter trapped him.

And he's probably pretty pissed.

"That's my guess," Eric said when I managed to put my thoughts to words. "Samarek had been biding his time for centuries. Patient. Careful. Waiting and planning for the right moment to burst free and rampage through the human world. And then some teenage girl slammed the door in his face and ruined centuries of preparation in a single moment."

"So he's angry," I said.

Eric almost smiled. "I think we can call that an understatement."

16

KATE

*W*hen I got to his room, Stuart was sitting on the edge of his bed, his head in his hands. He looked tired—the visions always left him drained—but when he lifted his head, his eyes were clear. Present. More like the Stuart I'd married than he'd been in months.

"Hey," I said softly. "We need to talk."

Something flickered across his face—wariness, maybe, or resignation. These days, "we need to talk" never led anywhere good.

"What's wrong?"

I sat down beside him, close enough that our shoulders almost touched.

Almost.

For half a second, I thought for sure I would cry. Then I drew a breath, reminded myself that I was a bad-ass Demon Hunter, and took the plunge.

"Marcus found something on Antonio's USB drive. Something about Eric. About this thing that happened twenty years ago in Rome."

He tilted his head. "I'm going to assume this isn't a happy story?"

"Kind of happy," I said with a grimace. "I mean, I'm not dead at the end."

For a moment, his features softened, and he put his hand on mine. "That is a happy ending."

I drew in a breath, almost scared to exhale. This was the closest I'd been emotionally to this man in months, and I just sat there, knowing we needed to get down to the meeting, but terrified of missing some shift in Stuart that would push him back to the *real and present* side of the equation.

"Tell me," he said, and I nodded like an eager puppy, thrilled to have him sticking his toe back into what had become our strange family's occupation.

I gave him the short version, of course. My optimism was only going so far. I filled him in on Samarek. The ritual. Saving my life—and then Allie coincidentally trapping the demon years later.

Stuart listened without interrupting, his face growing more closed with each revelation. When I finished, the silence stretched between us like a wire pulled too tight.

"So Eric made a deal with a demon to save your life," he finally said. "And now that demon wants revenge on Allie."

"Well, actually, yeah. That's the gist of it."

"And you're just finding this out now. Twenty years later."

"Stuart, please."

"How many more secrets, Kate?" His voice was quiet, but I heard the edge underneath. "How many more things about your past with Eric are going to come crawling out of the woodwork?"

"That's not fair."

"Isn't it?" He stood, moving away from me, and the distance felt like more than just physical space. "I'm not angry.

I'm just…tired. Tired of being the one who's always three steps behind. Tired of finding out that the life we built together has all these trap doors I didn't know existed."

I wanted to argue. Wanted to tell him that I hadn't known either, that Eric's secrets weren't my secrets. But the truth was more complicated than that, and we both knew it.

"We're calling a meeting," I said instead. "We need to figure out what we're dealing with and how to protect Allie."

Stuart nodded slowly. "I'll be there."

A knock at the door interrupted us, and I was more grateful than I should have been. Fran poked her head in, her expression apologetic. "Sorry to bother you, but Timmy's asking for his mom. He won't settle."

"I'll come." I stood, then hesitated. I wanted to reach for Stuart's hand, but I was afraid he'd just leave me hanging. "Get some rest if you can," I said to him instead. "Meeting's in fifteen minutes." Then I stepped out of the room without looking back, a strange sense of finality settling over me.

I forced myself to shake it off. Told myself that Stuart and I would get through this. Except I wasn't sure that we would. And there was some small, traitorous part of me that wasn't sad or scared. It was just quietly waiting to see where all of this would land.

I FOUND Timmy in his room, sitting up in bed with Boo Bear clutched against his chest. His dark hair was sticking up in all directions, and his lower lip had that telltale wobble that preceded either tears or a tantrum.

"Hey, baby." I scooped him up and settled into the rocking chair by the window, tucking him against me. "What's wrong? Bad dream?"

He shook his head, burying his face in my neck.

"Use your words, Timmy."

"Drew pictures," he mumbled.

"You drew pictures? That's great. You're such a good little artist."

"Miss Fran thinks they're scary."

"She said that?"

He shook his head. "But she thinks so."

I frowned, wishing I'd read a few more books on child psychology. Or, actually, any books.

Now, I glanced toward the small desk in the corner, where a few sheets of paper were scattered. Even from here, I could see they were more pictures of rectangles, except these were different. Dark. Heavy red and black crayon pressed hard into the paper.

"Can I see?"

He shook his head harder. "You won't like them either."

"I like everything you make," I said. "How about you try to sleep, and we'll look at them together in the morning?"

"Okay." He yawned, already relaxing against me. "Mommy?"

"Yeah, baby?"

"Is Daddy sad?"

My heart clenched. "No, baby. Daddy's just tired."

"Does Daddy need more hugs?"

God. Kids noticed everything.

"Maybe," I said, blinking back the sting in my eyes. "I think Daddy would love more hugs."

"I give him hugs tomorrow," Timmy said solemnly. "Big ones."

"That sounds perfect, baby."

Timmy seemed to accept that, his breathing evening out as sleep pulled him under. I held him for a while longer, rocking gently, watching the moonlight shift across his floor.

When I finally tucked him back into bed, I paused at the desk for a closer look at his drawings.

Red scribbles. Black shapes. A rectangle that seemed to have eyes and looked dark. Angry.

I grimaced, hoping this wasn't some psychological price he was paying because of the tension between me and Stuart.

That, however, wasn't something I could deal with now. So, I stepped away from the drawings, then left the room, pulling the door mostly closed behind me. I had a meeting to get to, and an ancient demon to worry about.

The drawings could wait.

I was on my way to find Allie when I heard voices coming from Laura's office. The door was cracked open, and I probably should have kept walking, but Laura's tone made me pause.

"I just think you need to be careful," she was saying. "New relationships are tricky even without adding stakes and demons into the mix."

"I know." Mindy hesitated. "It's just... He's really nice, you know? And cute. And he actually listens when you talk to him."

I leaned against the wall, shameless. Eavesdropping is a vital parenting skill. Anyone who tells you otherwise doesn't have teenagers.

Besides, Laura would tell me everything after the meeting, anyway.

"Those are good qualities," Laura said. "But you barely know Zane."

"I know. That's why I'm asking. I mean—"

She cut herself off, and for a moment, silence just hung

there. "It's just, well, I'm not supposed to say, but it's not me who likes him. It's Allie."

My heart stuttered.

Allie?

Allie and Zane?

Were there signs? Had I missed signs?

How could I have missed signs?

I mean, sure, she'd pulled him aside after a sparring session last week, but I assumed she was correcting his form. And, yes, they talked at meals, but she talked with everyone.

Still, he had come out of his shell around her. More so than he had with most of the others, except Mindy and Ren.

How on earth had I missed this?

I backed away from the door before they could catch me, my mind racing. Allie had Jared. Jared, who loved her. Jared, who'd been patient and steady and everything she needed.

Jared, whom I'd finally come to terms with being an ageless vampire who was dating my only daughter. Was she really going to throw him away for the new kid with the charming smile?

Except of course, she was. She was seventeen. Seventeen-year-olds made spectacularly bad romantic decisions.

Okay, that wasn't fair. I'd never regretted Eric. Not even after I learned all his secrets. Pissed, yes. Regretful, no.

Still, a hundred-year age difference raised a lot of red flags. I think any mom—or marriage counselor—would agree with that. But moving from Jared to Zane...?

Time for a mother-daughter talk. The meeting could wait five minutes. Some things were more important than apoca-lyptic revenge demons.

Okay, that probably wasn't true, but I pretended it was as I hurried to the training room where I found Allie running through forms with her stiletto. She moved like weaponized water—fluid, precise, deadly. My daughter. The girl who'd closed the gates of Hell.

The girl who was apparently on the verge of making what we moms like to call a Bad Life Choice.

I paused in the doorway, watching her. She was so much like Eric that sometimes it made my chest ache. The same intensity. The same single-minded focus. The same inability to do anything halfway.

Hopefully, her silence about her Zane crush wasn't a sign that she'd also inherited her father's annoying habit of keeping secrets he shouldn't keep.

"Allie. Got a minute?"

She finished her sequence and turned, barely winded. Her cheeks were flushed, her ponytail coming loose, and she looked so young I truly felt my heart squeeze.

Seventeen. How could my baby be seventeen?

I closed the door behind me, then moved to sit on the padded bench. "I wanted to have a mom/daughter talk."

Her eyebrows rose. "Okaaaay. That's not ominous at all."

I put my hand on her arm, supportive yet firm. "It's about Zane."

Something flickered across her face—surprise, maybe that I had a clue about her crush—but I pressed on before I could lose my nerve.

"Look, I get it," I said. "He's new, he's charming, he's good-looking. And at your age, it's natural to notice that."

Her brow was furrowed, but she didn't interrupt. I took that as a good sign, drew another breath, then dove back in. "The thing is, I know I was a little leery at first, but you have something real with Jared. Something most people never find. And I don't want you to throw that away because you're curious about the shiny new option."

Her eyes went wide, and her cheeks bloomed pink. "Um, Mom? I mean, what is this?"

"It's just that I know I wasn't always supportive of you and Jared. The age difference, the vampire thing—it's a lot. But you know that's changed, right? I've watched him with you, and I know he loves you. Really loves you. The kind of love that lasts."

She started to speak, but I held up a finger. "No, let me finish. I just want to say that before you do anything you can't take back, you need to think about what you'd be giving up."

She just gaped at me, her brow furrowed like it does when she's doing math.

Then her lips twitched, and her eyes got huge. "Oh. My. God. Mom."

She let the words hang as she laughed, and while I wanted to tell her that breaking Jared's heart was not funny, at the same time, I began to think that I'd gotten something wildly, terribly wrong.

"Mom," she said slowly, in the tone of someone savoring every word. "I don't have a crush on Zane."

"Okaaaay," I said, slowly. "Then why did Mindy tell Laura you did?"

"Um, hello? Because she has a crush on him."

"But she said you did."

"Well, duh. She probably wanted to feel out Aunt Laura about what she thinks of Zane." Allie was grinning now, clearly enjoying my discomfort far more than any loving daughter should.

"Oh." It took a second. Then…"*Oh!* So when I saw you two talking after training—"

"I was telling him to stop pulling his punches. He's good, but he's too careful. It's going to get him killed." She tilted her head, studying me with an expression that was uncomfortably knowing. "Did you really think I'd dump Jared?"

"No! I just thought maybe you were…confused. Or tempted. Or being an idiot."

"Mom." She put her hand on my arm, mimicking my earlier gesture with devastating accuracy. "I love Jared. Like, really love him. The kind of love that lasts." She grinned.

"You're enjoying this way too much."

"I really am."

I pressed my hand to my forehead. "I'm an idiot."

"Little bit." But her voice was fond. "For the record, I already know everything you said about Jared. But it's nice to hear you say it, too. I'll tell him you're a fan. Because you're right. He is good for me."

"He really is," I admitted.

"I know it's not easy for you," she said, her voice turning serious. And sounding much older than seventeen. "The age thing, the vampire thing, all of it. So thanks. For trying. But, you know, maybe don't say anything to Daddy. I mean, he knows, but he probably doesn't *know*. I'll tell him. Just not quite yet."

I laughed. "Fair enough," I said, standing and then pulling her up and into a hug. With a sigh, I breathed in the familiar scent of her shampoo and the faint metallic tang of the weapons she'd been handling. My baby girl, pretty much all grown up.

"I love you," I said, brushing away a tear. "Even when I'm being an oblivious idiot."

"Love you too, Mom." She hugged me back, then pulled away with a smirk. "Now, if you'll excuse me, I need to go tell Mindy that her secret crush isn't as secret as she thinks."

"Not yet. Tell her we're having a meeting. Library. Now."

"Oh." The teenager vanished, replaced by the Hunter. "What happened?"

"Nothing good," I said. "See you there. And hurry."

She didn't ask questions. She just nodded once and left, her footsteps quick and purposeful.

I stood alone in the training room, surrounded by

weapons and mirrors and the lingering warmth of my daughter's laughter.

And in a few minutes, I was going to have to tell her that an ancient demon was supremely pissed off and probably wanted her dead.

17

KATE

We gathered in the library because Eddie refused to move from his favorite chair, where he'd been curled up all day with Sherlock Holmes. We didn't argue. The rest of us had learned long ago that it was easier to bring the mountain to Mohammed.

Timmy was on the floor by the fireplace with his crayons, happily scribbling away while we talked. He was supposed to be in bed where I'd left him, but he'd woken up inconsolable, so Stuart had brought him down when he'd joined the meeting. Now Stuart was settled in the wingback by the window, looking more present than he had in days.

Laura and Cutter were on the loveseat, and Allie sat perched on the arm of Jared's chair while Mindy sat cross-legged on the floor beside them. Only Marcus and Eliza were missing. Eliza, because she'd gone back down to San Diego to help a friend move, and Marcus, because he was pulling Instructor duty and was outside in the cemetery putting the students through night training with various weapons.

Once everyone was settled, Eric and I took turns laying it

out—Samarek's freakish history. The ritual Gregory Mathes had performed twenty years ago, calling on that dangerous and powerful demon to perform a ritual that used Eric's blood and saved my life.

And our certainty that Samarek was back—his mark on Antonio had been the demon's calling card.

When we finished, the room was silent.

"But why is it here?" Cutter finally asked. "Revenge on Eric for using his magic?"

"Partly," Eric said. "But I think the bigger target is Allie."

All eyes shifted to my daughter.

"She closed the gates of hell," Eric continued. "Locked Samarek and a huge number of hibernating demons on the wrong side. That's not something he's going to forget."

"Or forgive," Eddie added grimly.

"But it's more than revenge." Eric's jaw tightened. "Allie's powerful. Samarek would want that power for himself. To use. To control."

"So I'm what? A trophy and a weapon?" Allie's voice was flat, but I could see the fear beneath it.

"You're a threat," I said. "And a prize. That's a dangerous combination."

"Great." She crossed her arms. "So we know he wants me dead or captured. What we don't know is how he plans to get to me. He's stuck in hell, right? That's the whole point of closing the gates."

"That's what I've been researching," Mindy said. I remembered that she'd been the one to hack the USB and had been working with Marcus on sorting everything out. Considering how gifted she was at research, I wasn't surprised she was already on the trail.

"I've been going through everything Antonio compiled, and there's this one bit in his notes. Hang on. She pulled out her tablet, scrolling until she found what she was looking for.

"Here. This text's about Samarek specifically. It calls him *Pons Fabricator.*"

"Bridge builder," Eric translated, leaning forward.

"Exactly. According to this, Samarek is known for creating bridges between realms. Except, I don't think you can build a bridge out of hell from the inside."

"So he's pissed," Eric said, nodding slowly. "Allie locked him in the one place he couldn't escape. Not from the inside, anyway. He's immortal, so eventually he'd find a way. But he wants revenge. So he's doubling down on finding an exit point to get past that closed gate."

"By building a bridge," I said, nodding slowly as all that settled in my mind. "And if he can't build it from inside hell, he's going to try to figure out a way to influence demons on this side to do his bidding and construct the thing."

"Yes," Allie whispered, her eyes going wide. "But it's not a bridge." She looked between me and her father. "It's a door."

She nodded to Timmy and the picture he was drawing. "Lots of little kids sense weird stuff, you see it all the time in haunted house lore. They grow out of it, but the little ones know. I think Timmy's drawing the door that Samarek's going to come through."

"Going to," I whispered, thinking about the demon attack at Allie's party. "What if he's already succeeded?"

I crossed to my son and knelt down beside him. "Hey, baby. That's a pretty picture."

"It's a door," he said without looking up.

"I see that. You've been drawing a lot of doors lately."

"Uh-huh."

"Where do you see this door, sweetheart? Is it somewhere in the house?"

He shook his head, crayon still moving. "In my head. I see it when I close my eyes sometimes." He finally looked up at me, his expression impossibly innocent. "It's in the dark place. Where the knocking man waits."

I couldn't breathe. Couldn't move.

"What knocking man, baby?"

"He knocks and knocks. He's mad." Timmy's lower lip trembled. "He wants to come through the door and take the girl away."

Allie.

I met Eric's eyes, then Stuart's, who leaned forward, then tossed his head violently back. "The seed of she who closed the gate." His voice was a low rumble. "The child of he who called me forth. Used, then hid. She who bore the key. From the blood of an innocent, I come, and all three shall feel the pain of my vengeance and the hell-traitor shall be mine."

The words stopped and Stuart slumped forward, landing on the carpet in a heap.

"Daddy!" Timmy ran to his father. "Mommy! Mommy!"

I was there in a second, holding Timmy, looking to Allie and Eric for help, but they were already moving. Allie to take and comfort Timmy, Eric to help me get Stuart back in his chair as he woke up, confused and disoriented.

"Another one?"

"I'll tell you about it later. Just rest now."

"I'll take him upstairs," Marcus said. "You should sleep," he added to Stuart. "Keep talking. I'll catch up."

Then he was walking Stuart away and I had to fight the urge to go with him. Not only because I had a job to do here and knew perfectly well Marcus could handle this. But also because I feared that Stuart wouldn't want me there at all.

For a moment, no one spoke. Then Mindy said, "*The seed of she who closed the gate.* That's got to be Allie, right?"

I looked at Allie, who nodded. "Yeah, got there on my own."

Mindy consulted her ever-present tablet. "Right. And

then he said, *The child of he who called me forth. Used, then hid. She who bore the key.*"

"Well, Allie must be the key," Laura said. "Because keys make things lock."

I looked at the others, and everyone nodded.

"And I'm the one who bore her," I said, meeting Allie's eyes. "So he's looking for vengeance against the three of us."

"How?" Allie asked.

For a moment we all just looked at each other. "I guess we won't know until we know," Eric finally said. "We need to be ready for anything."

I almost smiled. "So what else is new?"

"He must be building a portal somewhere here," Eric said. "Somehow, he's got help on this side, and he's trying his damnedest to get through."

"Then we need to find that thing pronto," Eddie said. "Because if he comes through, we'll all end up in hell with him."

"The dark place," Allie murmured. Then her head snapped up. "Wait. Mindy, what was that prophecy? The one Stuart made at orientation. The binding enchantment thing."

"Hang on...got it. The door opens below that which binds enchantment," Mindy recited. "The vessel of light that is shadowed. Blood calls to blood. The ruby bleeds."

"Below that which binds enchantment," Eric repeated. "Something that binds. Contains. Holds magic in check."

"The whole mansion was demonic once," I said slowly. "Monroe's experiments. But we cleansed it. Father Corletti blessed every room."

"Every room, including the one that was already holy," Eddie said, sitting up straighter in his chair. "The Safe Room."

That had to be it. The Safe Room was exactly what it sounded like, only it was designed to protect its inhabitants from bad guys both human and demonic, which was why the walls were reinforced not just with steel but with relics. Actual saints' bones, sealed into the foundation and mixed into the mortar.

"Saints' bones bind enchantment," Eric said. "Stuart's vision must be referring to that. So what we're looking for is below it. Below the Safe Room."

"That makes sense," Laura said. "There are old servant passages under the house, right? They must go pretty much everywhere."

"He's building a door right under our feet," Allie said, her voice hard. "A way to reach through and grab us. Me and Mom and Daddy."

"We won't let him," Cutter said.

"First task is finding the portal," I said, standing, now hungry for action. Needing to do something—anything—to protect my daughter.

"Then we figure out how to destroy it and keep Samarek away from you three. And trapped in hell," Eddie said.

"Kate—" Eric caught my arm.

"I know," I said. "We don't know what we're walking into. But time is running out. We need to go careful, go armed, and go together. But, we also need to go now."

I looked around the room. "Stuart, Eddie—stay here with Timmy. Get all the kids in here, too, along with Marcus and Fran and all the staff. Everyone armed, just in case. Protect the students."

"I'm going into the basement," Allie said. It wasn't a question.

I wanted to argue. Wanted to lock her in the Safe Room and never let her out. She was the one Samarek truly wanted, after all. I was certain of it. She was the one he'd torture first, because that would hurt both Eric and me.

But at the same time, for all those reasons, she needed to

come, too. Because along with Jared, she was the strongest warrior we had.

"Fine. But you stay behind me and your father. Jared," I added, "you're with us." A few minutes later, once I was sure everyone not going under the house was safe in the library, I glanced at our little group. "All right, then. Time to see what's hiding under our noses."

18

ALLIE

The basement stairs creaked under our feet, each step taking us deeper into the dark.

Dad went first, a flashlight in one hand and a blade in the other. Mom followed close behind, and Jared's hand found mine as we brought up the rear.

The door opens below that which binds enchantment.

Just a little bit farther, and we'd be directly under the Safe Room. Or, at least, I think we would. Please, please, let us not have guessed wrong or somehow veered off course in this dark and creepy basement.

"How far back do these passages go?" I asked, keeping my voice low. "We must be getting close, right?"

"No idea," Mom admitted. "I've never had a reason to come down here. Who knows what these walls have seen? Or what they hide."

A lovely thought.

The thing is, no one really knew what Theophilis did to this house—or what havoc Lilith's break-in had wreaked back before this building housed Forza.

For that matter, Stuart and his business partners had done

work before they tried to sell the place, and they could have shifted bits heavy with mojo and then sent them to the county dump.

After all, they'd made a lot of changes before Mom got the idea for Forza West.

In other words, none of us had a clue as to what was actually down here.

The passage narrowed as we moved deeper. The walls changed from drywall to stone, the floor from concrete to packed earth. The air grew colder, damper, and it smelled like something old. Something that had been waiting.

"There." Dad stopped, his flashlight landing on a wooden door set into the stone. Heavy oak planks bound with rusted iron. "That shouldn't be here."

"What do you mean?" Jared asked.

"I've seen the original blueprints. There's not supposed to be a doorway here." He examined the door without touching it. "Someone added this."

"Want me to text Stuart?" I asked.

"No need." Dad pointed at the door. "See?"

I studied the door in the dim glow of his flashlight.

No handle. No visible hinges. Just a symbol carved into the wood at eye level—layers of intersecting lines and curves that looked almost like a fingerprint. I drew in a breath, then whispered, "Samarek's mark."

At least we knew we were in the right place.

"So what do we do?" Mom asked. "Knock?"

The door swung open.

"Well, okay then," Mom murmured.

Beyond the door lay darkness so complete that the glow from Dad's flashlight got swallowed three feet past the threshold.

"Jared?"

"I can't see, either," he said. "Haven't run into that before. An enchantment?"

"Well, this isn't ominous at all," I muttered.

Of course, we stepped through anyway.

The room was wrong. Too large—much larger than the space above would allow. The ceiling disappeared into shadow, and the walls curved in ways that made my eyes hurt and gave the sense that we were walking and tilting all at the same time. This wasn't the basement anymore. This was somewhere else. Somewhere that didn't care about physics or blueprints or the rules of the normal world.

Dad's flashlight swept the room, and my heart stopped.

Trevor.

He lay on his back in the center of the room, arms flung out to his sides, his shirt dark and wet with blood. A deep wound gaped across his throat. His wrists had been sliced open, too.

"Oh God," Mom whispered.

For one horrible second, I couldn't move. Couldn't think. All I could do was stare at the boy I'd trained beside just yesterday, now lying broken and dead on the cold stone floor.

Then Jared's hand tightened around mine, and something clicked into place. I gasped, blinking back tears as I forced myself to be strong. To look around. To be a Hunter and assess the situation.

And to stay alive.

I made myself breathe. In. Out. In. Out.

With effort, I pushed down the scream building in my chest. There would be time to fall apart later. Right now, I needed to see. To understand.

Trevor's eyes were open, staring at nothing. Gone. Whatever spark that had made him Trevor—angry, guarded, hurting Trevor—had left.

But it wasn't just his body that made my stomach lurch. It was what lay beneath him.

He'd been placed on top of something. A shape on the floor, outlined in pulsing red light. Door-shaped. And on one side, two spheres glowed like freakish doorknobs.

Like Timmy's drawings.

The portal.

My knees went weak. All those pictures. All those doors Timmy had been drawing obsessively for weeks. He'd been seeing this. This exact thing.

Trevor's blood oozed away from him, as if called to seep into the door-shape's outline. And with each drop of ruby red blood, the light pulsed brighter. Hungrier.

The thing was feeding. Feeding on him. On his death.

I thought I might be sick.

A circle of dirt surrounded him, glowing faintly, as if it was keeping him trapped while the life drained out of him.

But the worst part—the part that made me want to look away and never stop looking at the same time—was his left hand. Someone had painted symbols on his palm in what looked like his own blood. Geometric markings, intricate and deliberate. The same layered lines and curves as Samarek's mark on the door.

He'd been marked. Claimed.

Used.

Mom's phone buzzed, and I jumped so hard I nearly screamed. She glanced at it, her face going pale as she tapped out a reply. "Trevor broke away from the group twenty minutes ago. They've been searching." She looked at the body. "They're too late."

Twenty minutes. He'd been alive just twenty minutes ago. Walking around. Breathing. And now—

I sucked in air and forced myself to keep my shit together

by squeezing Jared's hand so hard it's a wonder I didn't crush his bones.

Trevor. Lying there like a sacrifice.

Because that's exactly what he was. *"The blood of an innocent,"* I murmured.

Dad moved first, stepping carefully around the dirt circle and the glowing edge of the portal, his face a mask I recognized. A Hunter's face. The one that let you function when everything inside you was screaming.

"Eric," Mom whispered. "Be careful."

He didn't answer. Just knelt beside Trevor's body and pressed his fingers to Trevor's neck. Checking for a pulse we all knew wouldn't be there.

"No pulse," he said flatly. "But he's still warm. This just happened. Minutes ago, maybe."

Minutes. We'd missed him by minutes.

"The blood's still flowing," Jared said quietly. "The portal's still feeding."

I made myself step closer. Made myself really look at Trevor's face, even though every instinct screamed at me to turn away. There was something in his expression that looked almost like surprise. Whatever he'd thought was going to happen down here, dying hadn't been part of the plan.

I looked at the symbols on his left palm. "Those markings... Did he draw them? Or did someone put them on him? Did he come down here willingly?"

"It fits." Mom's voice was hollow, and I could hear her own struggle to stay in Hunter mode. "He broke away from the group tonight despite knowing we were facing a real threat. And his attitude... We may never know."

"What if he was working with someone?" I asked. "What if he thought he was getting something out of this?"

"And when he'd served his purpose..." Dad didn't finish the sentence. He didn't have to.

I shuddered, then leaned against Jared as his arm tightened protectively around me. I'd seen death before. I'd caused death before—demon death, sure, but I'd felt bodies go limp under my hands, watched the light leave eyes that had once been human before something else moved in. I'd faced down Hell itself and walked away.

But this was different.

Trevor was seventeen. Same as me. He'd arrived three weeks ago with anger radiating off him like heat, and I'd been so wrapped up in my own problems—the prophecy, Samarek, my complicated family—that I hadn't even tried to see past his hostility to whatever was underneath. I'd written him off as difficult, and someone had used that. Used the fact that none of us had really seen him.

Now I'd never get the chance to know him. Never get to find out what he was so angry about, or what he might have become if someone had just bothered to reach past his walls.

"Allie." Jared's voice was soft. His hand rested on my shoulder. "It wasn't your fault."

"It was," I said. "At least a little. But I'll be okay," I said. Because I had to be. Because that's part of who I was now. The girl who kept going. The girl who didn't get to fall apart until the job was done.

I sucked in a breath and looked between the three of them. "Something's still wrong," I said. "How did whoever did this know the portal was here? I mean, someone had to lure him down here. Had to cut him. It wasn't Samarek. He's still bound.

Mom and Dad exchanged a look. "Still bound? Are you sure?"

I nodded, feeling a little icky about that tidbit of knowledge. "I can feel him," I said, as Jared took my hand, giving it a supportive squeeze. "I can't explain it, but I'm sure. The door isn't open for him. He's still trapped, but he's calling to his minions in this realm to come. To bring sacrifices to make the cracks bigger so the portal will open for him." I shrugged. "Blood. He needs more. And we have a supply of sacrifices right upstairs." I looked between the two of them. "We have to figure out how to seal this thing back up. And," I added, "we need to do it fast."

"We do," Daddy said. "And we need to know how Trevor was lured down here, especially if it was someone upstairs."

"No way," I said. "We know them all." Which, of course, was just a reflex. Because we didn't. No one ever truly knows anyone but themselves. And most people aren't even that aware. But. I didn't think it was anyone on the staff or any student from last year. And I didn't want to think it could be Zane or Sophie. I'd seen them fight at my party, and both kicked demon ass.

It had to be an outsider. Because if it wasn't, then Trevor's killer was someone we trusted. Someone who walked these halls, ate at our table, trained beside us.

Someone who was probably still up there right now, pretending to be scared about what would come next.

My tears fell to the ground, and the portal pulsed a deep ruby red. Brighter. Hungrier. Like it was feeding on my grief too. Taking everything it could get.

I wiped my face angrily. I wasn't going to give it anything else.

"We need to get him out of here," Mom said, her voice cracking just slightly before she steadied it. "For that matter, we need to all get away from this portal."

But I couldn't move. Not yet. I stood watching it pulse like a perverted heartbeat, almost mesmerized by the way the door seemed to shrink inside the glowing frame, letting an eerie red light leak out around the sides to cast unnatural geometric splashes of light on the dingy walls.

"It's not fully open," I whispered. "But it wants to be."

Mom nodded, looking a little ill. "How long do you think?"

"Depends on how long it takes to lure another sacrifice," Daddy said. "Never if I have any say in it."

"I like the sound of never," I said.

Daddy grimaced. "Chances are it will be sooner than that. Unless we close it, those pulses are like a demon magnet, luring all sorts of demons our way. They'll kill whoever stands in their way and drag whoever they can to the portal so they can kill them there. We need to tell the kids to be prepared to fight whatever's coming. And we need to figure out how to close the portal."

"How long?" Jared asked.

Daddy shook his head. "No idea. But if I had to guess, I'd say San Diablo will be overrun within an hour of that portal fully opening."

"Maybe I can close it," I said. "I've done it before." It didn't feel the same. Before, I felt the power flowing through me. Now, I just felt hope.

Maybe that would be enough.

With that thought bolstering me, I took my knife from my pocket, slit my palm, and pressed it to the pulsing rectangle, my mind and body braced for torment as the portal fought back.

Except nothing happened.

The portal continued to pulse, wanting and craving. My blood just sat there on the surface, doing absolutely nothing.

I met Daddy's eyes. "You try it."

I could tell from his expression he didn't think he'd do any better, but he did have the connection to Samarek, so I crossed my fingers as he bled on the portal.

Nothing.

"There has to be a way," I said.

Jared took my hand. "We'll find it."

"And we need to find it fast," Mom said. "But no pressure."

I actually laughed, a tiny bit, anyway. And it felt good.

"Let's get back up," Mom said. "We need to brief everyone. And I want to know they're all safe."

"We'll figure it out," Jared said as he wrapped a handkerchief around my hand. And we'll stop it."

"Promise?"

"Yes," he said, but we both knew that might be a promise he wouldn't be able to keep.

19

KATE

"Trevor is dead."

I didn't soften it. These kids had signed up to hunt demons, and they deserved to be treated like the warriors they were training to become.

The words hit the room like a slap, all the students and staff gaping at me like they couldn't understand a word I was saying. Like it couldn't be true.

I wished it weren't. But it was real. It was so very, very real.

I heard a quick sob as Sophie's breath caught, and I saw Ana reaching for her hand, tears running down her cheeks. Beside them, Ren went pale as a ghost. I wanted to cry, too. To sink down and hug my knees to my chest. But I couldn't. Not now. Not yet.

"He was murdered," I continued, forcing my voice to sound strong. "His body was found in the basement, laid out on a portal hidden beneath this house."

"A portal?" Mindy's voice came out reedy and thin. "Like...a door? To where?"

"To Hell," Eric said. "Or close enough." He moved to

stand beside me, his presence steadying. "The demon responsible is called Samarek. He's ancient. Powerful. And he's been planning this for a very long time."

I watched their faces as the information landed. Their eyes showed fear even as their hands fisted and their bodies tightened. They wanted payback.

Good. So did I.

Sophie had drawn her knees up, making herself small, but her hands were fisted. Ren's jaw was tight, his hands clenched on his thighs. Ana sat very still, the way people do when they're trying not to shake apart.

Mindy had tears streaming silently down her cheeks. She didn't bother wiping them away.

In the corner of the couch, Zane hugged himself, but was otherwise absolutely still. He looked like a soft wind could break him. As if he didn't want to believe me and didn't have a clue how to carry the weight of it all.

"How?" The question came from Ana. She sat rigid beside Ren, her hand locked so tightly in his that her knuckles had gone white. "How did he die?"

I hesitated. They needed to know, but the details were brutal.

"His throat was cut," Eric said, sparing me. "His blood fed the portal. Made it stronger."

Ana made a small, wounded sound as Sophie bit her lower lip and the others fidgeted.

"That's why he was down there?" Ren asked. "Someone...someone took him down there to kill him?"

"We don't know," I said honestly. "Not yet. There were ritual marks on his hands—demonic marks that are tied to a demon called Samarek."

I watched their faces as I said the demon's name, but none showed any sign of recognition. "We don't know if he made the marks himself to call the demon, or if the demon marked him before sacrificing him."

"Trevor wouldn't—" Sophie started, then stopped. Her face crumpled. "He was so angry all the time. But he wasn't...he wouldn't..."

Zane lifted his head. His eyes were red-rimmed, and when he spoke, his voice cracked. "He saved Timmy. At the party. When the demons attacked, Trevor grabbed Timmy and got him inside. He wasn't the way he came off. Not really."

"No," I agreed softly. "He wasn't."

Another silence. Longer this time and broken only by Ana and Sophie's soft sobs.

"So what do we do?" The question came from Ren. His voice wobbled, but he lifted his chin. "How do we stop it?"

"All of the staff is working on that. Forza knows what's happening. We're expecting backup, but I won't lie to you— things may move faster than help can arrive."

"We're helping, too, right?" Sophie's voice shook, but there was steel underneath the fear. "Trevor wouldn't have summoned a demon on purpose. Someone must have tricked him. And we're not going to let them get away with it."

One by one, the others nodded. Mindy wiped her face with her sleeve and sat up straighter. Ren unclenched his fists. Ana put her arm around Sophie and pulled her close.

Zane just stared at the floor, his jaw working like he was fighting to hold himself together.

"This is the job," I said. "But fear can get you killed, so if anyone wants to walk away now, there'll be no judgment. No shame. You newbies aren't trained for something like this. Not yet."

For a moment, there was total silence. Then little Sophie stood, her chin lifted.

"I'm staying," she said. "He would have fought for us, and I'm going to fight for him."

"Me, too," said Ren, then Ana, too, adding a curt, "duh," to punctuate her statement.

One by one, they all stood until only Zane was still seated. Then he stood, too, and something in his expression made my heart ache. Such grief there. Such guilt. The look of someone who wished they could have done something, anything, to change what had happened.

"Trevor could be an ass," he said. "But he didn't deserve what he got. I'm staying."

I nodded, hoping they could all see how full my heart was with pride.

I was about to dive back into instructions when one more voice chimed in. "I'm staying, too," Eliza said from the doorway, looking breathless from hurrying. "Or, I guess, I'm coming back." She met my eyes and shrugged. "My friend's got a houseful of family helping her cope. After Mindy texted, I figured I should come back and help the family I have."

I nodded, brushing away a tear, then drew a breath and looked out at all their faces.

"Here's what happens next," I said, my voice rough with emotion. "Everyone's in research mode—Eric will brief you on Forza's past interactions with Samarek and assign you specific areas to research. Combat training continues, but we're stepping it up. And nobody—I mean nobody—goes near the basement. Not the door, not the stairs, not even that hallway. The portal is contained for now, but it's hungry. It wants to be fed. Don't give it the chance."

I turned to look at Fran. "You can go, or you and Elena can stay here, and we'll reinforce your room. Either way, Timmy stays."

I hated saying that—I wanted to send my baby far away where he could stay safe while all this went down. But Samarek wanted to claim his own, and it was his power that had healed me all those years ago. And like a scary mob boss, he just might take my kid as payment.

Until Samarek was killed or contained, that meant that Timmy was vulnerable in the world.

"We're staying," she said. "This is our home now, too, and I'll do what I can. Even if that means keeping me and the kids locked in a room so you guys can kick demon ass."

I couldn't help my grin. "That sounds about right."

I gave her a hug, then took a moment to breathe, trying to get organized. That's when I saw Stuart leaning against the wall. His eyes found mine, but I didn't have a clue what he was thinking.

"And one more thing." I waited until I had everyone's attention. "Watch each other's backs. If you see anything suspicious—anything at all—you come to Eric or me immediately. Understood?"

More nods, though these were slower. Warier. I hated putting that seed of doubt in their minds, but they needed to be careful. We all did.

"Meeting's over. Eddie, Laura—get them started. I want to know what we're dealing with before sunset."

The students rose slowly, reluctantly, like they weren't quite ready to leave the safety of the group. Mindy had her arm around Sophie. Ren and Ana walked close together, shoulders almost touching. Eliza fell into step beside them, her expression grim and protective.

Allie lingered, catching my eye with a question in her gaze. I shook my head slightly. *Later.* She nodded once, then let Jared guide her out of the common room, his hand steady on the small of her back.

The room emptied.

Almost.

Zane had stood with the others, had moved toward the

door with them. But now he stood just inside the threshold, watching the last of his classmates disappear down the hall, his hands shoved deep in his pockets.

When the footsteps faded, he turned back to face us. His face was ashen.

"I need to talk to you," he said. His voice was barely above a whisper. "Both of you. Please."

I exchanged a glance with Eric. His shoulders rose slightly, just as clueless as I was.

"All right," I said, then shut the door.

"What's on your mind?"

He didn't answer me right away. His hands were trembling—actually trembling—and he shoved them in his pockets to hide it. The movement was so achingly young that my chest tightened. This wasn't the confident, charming boy who'd walked into Forza West with easy jokes and a practiced smile. This was a terrified teenager.

"It's okay," Eric said. "Whatever it is, the hardest part is always the first word."

Zane nodded. "I—it's just—I don't know how to say this." His voice cracked on the last word. "I've been trying to figure out the words and there aren't any good ones."

Eric and I exchanged a glance. I had no idea where this was going, but every instinct I'd honed over the years screamed that I wasn't going to like it.

"Just say it," Eric said. His voice was gentle but firm. "Whatever it is, just get it out."

Zane took a breath. Held it. Let it out slowly, like a man standing on a ledge trying to talk himself into jumping.

"Samarek is my father."

The words detonated in the quiet room.

I stared at him. More accurately, I gaped at him. My brain stuttered, trying and failing to process what I'd just heard. *Samarek.* The demon who'd been hunting my family. The ancient evil trying to claw his way through the portal in our basement. And this kid. This student we'd welcomed into our school, fed at our table, trusted with our children—

He was its *son?*

Eric had gone completely still in his chair. The kind of stillness that preceded violence.

Eddie was on his feet. "Son of a—"

"Eddie." Eric's voice cut through like a blade. "Let him talk."

"Let him talk? He just admitted he's the spawn of the thing trying to destroy us!"

"Which is exactly why we need to hear what he has to say." Eric's eyes never left Zane, and I saw the anger there, and the fear. But I also saw understanding. Eric knew a bit about having ties to a demon. "Keep going."

Allie hadn't moved from her spot by the door, but her face had gone pale. She was staring at Zane as if she'd never seen him before. Like everything she thought she knew had just shattered.

"Explain," I said, my voice cold.

Zane flinched as if I'd slapped him. Good. Let him flinch. Let him feel some fraction of the fear Trevor must have felt.

But even as I thought it, another part of me saw the way his shoulders were curving inward, the way his whole body seemed to be trying to make itself smaller. The way he couldn't meet my eyes.

"He's been using me. Since I was ten." Zane's voice had dropped to barely above a whisper. "Small things at first. Deliver a message to someone. Leave a mark on a door. I didn't know what any of it meant. I didn't even know what he *was*, not really. He just...he was my dad. The dad who'd never been around, who showed up out of nowhere when I turned nine and said he wanted to be part of my life."

He laughed, and the sound was so hollow, so utterly

devoid of humor, that something in my chest cracked despite my fury.

"My mom was thrilled. We were flat broke, and she'd been a single parent my whole life, working two jobs, barely keeping us afloat. And suddenly, this guy she'd been with once was offering to help. She didn't ask questions. Neither did I. We were both so goddamn desperate to believe."

"He had you deliver messages," Eric said, his voice tight. "What kind?"

"Weird stuff. Tell the man at the bookstore that the shipment is delayed. Leave this symbol on the door of some church." Zane spread his hands. "I didn't understand any of it. But when I did what he asked, things were easier. Better. My mom got a promotion she'd been passed over for three times. I aced a test I hadn't studied for. Little things. Good things."

His face darkened.

"And when I didn't..."

He trailed off. His jaw tightened, and I watched him wrestle with something—some memory he didn't want to share but knew he had to.

"What happened when you didn't?" I pressed.

"My mom got sick once. Really sick." His voice had gone hoarse. "The doctors couldn't figure out what was wrong. She was in the hospital for a week, and they kept running tests, but nothing made sense. Nothing worked. She was dying, and I couldn't—I didn't—" He broke off, breathing hard. "There was something he'd asked me to do. Something I'd been putting off because it felt wrong. I did it." Zane's hands were shaking again. "She was fine the next day. Just...*fine*. Like nothing had happened. The doctors called it a miracle."

The silence that followed was suffocating. I could hear the old house settling around us, creaks and groans that usually faded into background noise but now seemed deafening.

"He was conditioning you," Eric said quietly.

"I know that now. But I was a kid, and I wanted a dad. Especially after Mom was killed. I was fourteen. Car accident. That's when I got really tight with Sam—that's what he called himself as my dad."

He dragged his fingers through his hair. "I should have figured it out by then. It shouldn't have been so easy for a kid to keep an apartment. I never had a clue, though."

"Convenient," Eddie muttered. "Do whatever Daddy wants and blame it on manipulation."

"Eddie," I warned.

"No, he's right." Zane's voice was steady now, steadier than it had any right to be. "It is convenient. It's also true. Both things can be real at the same time."

Zane met my eyes for the first time since his confession had started. What I saw there wasn't defiance or excuses or even hope. It was pure, unvarnished self-loathing.

"I didn't know what he was. I thought maybe he was in the mob, or some kind of secret society. And I told myself the stuff he asked me to do wasn't that bad. I mean, I never hurt anyone—or at least, I don't think it did. And he told me about the good things he did. About how he could save lives. How he could heal."

I stiffened, thinking about Eric and the rite that had saved me.

"I told myself he was some kind of immortal protector," Zane continued. "Some awesome guy getting down and dirty in disguise as he worked behind the scenes to fight evil." His voice cracked. "How pathetic is that? A teenager still believing in fairy tales."

I thought about Allie. About how badly she'd wanted to believe the best of people, even when the evidence pointed elsewhere. About how easy it was, when you were young and desperate and lonely, to believe in simple narratives. Good guys and bad guys. Heroes and villains. Fathers who loved you.

"Not pathetic," I said, and the words surprised me. "Human."

Zane looked at me like I'd spoken a foreign language. Like kindness was the last thing he'd expected—and the one thing he couldn't handle.

He managed a small smile, then nodded. "He disappeared almost two years ago," he said, the timeline matching when Allie had closed the gate. "And even though I'd told myself he was this noble guy, I was secretly relieved. I wanted him gone."

He sucked in a breath. "But now he wants out. Wherever he's stuck, he's managed to get little bits out. Just thoughts, maybe telepathy. I don't know. But he talks to me. Not often, but he does."

"He told you how to open the portal."

He nodded, looking even more miserable.

"Trevor," Eric said, and the name landed between us like a blade.

Zane's whole body contracted. Shoulders curving in, head dropping, arms wrapping around himself like he could physically hold himself together. When he spoke, his voice was wrecked.

"Sam told me to mark him. Said the boy needed to be marked. For later." His hands came up, pressing against his face, and his next words were muffled, broken. "I didn't know what it meant. I thought it was protection, maybe. Or—I don't know."

His voice cracked completely. He stood there, this kid who'd walked into our school with easy confidence and a charming smile, and he shattered in front of us.

"I didn't know it would kill him. I swear to God, I didn't know his blood would open—that he would—that I was—"

He couldn't finish. Silent sobs wracked his body, and he pressed his hands harder against his face like he could push the grief back inside.

"Bullshit." Eddie's voice was hard. "You expect us to believe that load of horseshit?"

"I believe him."

Everyone turned to look at Eric. He'd been silent since Zane started talking about Trevor, his face unreadable. But now he stepped forward. "I know what it's like," Eric said, his voice low. "To have something inside you that you didn't ask for. Something that makes you do things you don't understand. Things you can't stop."

Zane stared at him.

Eric turned to look at me and Allie. "You both saw what I did when that fucker got unbound inside me. I was horrible, and most horrible of all to both of you."

He wasn't wrong.

"I almost hurt the people I love most," he told Zane. "My daughter. Her mother. I wasn't in control. I was a passenger in my own body, watching myself become a monster."

The room had gone very still.

"You didn't choose this," Eric continued. "You didn't have a choice in what he did to you, or what he made you carry, or what he turned you into while you're too young and too desperate and too goddamn trusting to know any better. The only thing you get to choose is what you do next."

Allie moved then, stepping forward to stand near Zane. She didn't touch him, didn't offer comfort exactly, but she was there. Present.

"I get it too," she said quietly. "I know what it's like to carry something inside you that scares you. To wonder if you're dangerous. To have people look at you and see a threat instead of a person." She glanced at Eric, then back at Zane. "The only difference between us is that I had people who told me the truth. Who helped me understand what I was dealing with. You had a demon whispering lies."

Zane stared at her like she'd thrown him a lifeline he didn't deserve.

And I felt it all.

Disgust, hot and thick in my throat—because this boy had marked one of my students for death, had helped that *thing* in my basement claim a child's life, and no amount of "I didn't know" would ever bring Trevor back.

Understanding, bitter as it was—because I'd seen what Eric had gone through, too.

Pride, strange and unexpected, because it took courage to stand in front of us and confess. To hand us a loaded weapon and wait to see if we'd use it. Most people ran from their sins. This kid was running toward accountability.

Pride in my daughter, too. For seeing past her own fear to recognize a kindred spirit.

And sadness. God, the sadness. Because there was no fixing this. No time machine, no way to unsay the words that had damned Trevor or undo the mark that had killed him. The past was written in blood, and all any of us could do was carry the weight of it forward.

Eric took a step closer to Zane, waiting until the boy's sobs had quieted to ragged breathing. Until the hands dropped, and the blotchy, tear-streaked face was visible.

"Look at me," Eric said.

Zane looked. He was expecting condemnation—I could see it in the set of his jaw, the way he braced himself.

"I spent my childhood as a lab rat," Eric said, his voice low and steady. "A priest named Donnelly thought he could create the perfect Demon Hunter. He experimented on me, even before my birth. Injected me with things. Put something inside me I didn't know about until years later—demonic essence that I carried without understanding, and which I passed to my daughter without meaning to. Which was exactly Donnelly's end game."

Zane stared at him.

"You don't get to choose your father," Eric continued. "You don't get to choose what he does to you, or what he makes you carry, or what he turns you into while you're too young and too desperate and too goddamn trusting to know any better. The only thing you get to choose is what you do next."

"But Trevor—"

"Is dead." The words were gentle despite their brutality. "And that's a weight you'll carry for the rest of your life. Every day. Every night when you can't sleep. Every time you see a kid who reminds you of him." Eric's voice dropped. "I know. Believe me, I know. But carrying the weight doesn't mean you have to drown in it. It doesn't mean you don't get to keep fighting."

Something passed between them—this man who'd spent decades wrestling with the things that had been done to him and the boy who was just beginning to understand the shape of his own cage.

"Why tell us?" I asked. "Why now?"

Zane turned to me, and I saw the answer in his face before he spoke.

"Because I never thought I could tell *anyone*. Who was going to believe me? The cops? They'd think I was insane. A priest? They might burn me at the stake. My friends?" He laughed, hollow and exhausted. "What friends?"

He spread his hands helplessly.

"But you people get it, and a lot deeper than I thought, too. You actually know that demons are real, that my father is a monster, that the marks I made weren't just creepy requests from a weird dad. For the first time in my life, telling the truth doesn't make me sound crazy. It just makes me sound like what I am."

"Which is?" I asked.

"A weapon," he said quietly, reminding me that Allie had once called herself that. "But they pointed me at the wrong target." He straightened slightly. Not much—he was still hollowed out, wrecked, barely holding together—but enough. Enough to meet my eyes without flinching.

"I'm done being his puppet. Whatever you want me to do, I'll do it. Lock me up. Use me as bait. Kill me if you think that's safer." His voice steadied. "I don't care. I just want to help stop him. I want Trevor's death to mean something."

The room fell silent. I looked at Eric. He looked at me. Eddie was still scowling, but some of the rage had drained out of his posture. Allie stood with her arms crossed, watching Zane with an expression I couldn't quite read.

There was a conversation happening between Eric and me that didn't need words. Years of fighting together, of trusting each other's judgment, of making impossible calls in impossible situations. I knew what he was thinking. He knew what I was thinking.

"Here's what's going to happen," I said finally. "You stay, but we tell the others the truth. You help us. But Jared is going to be keeping a close eye on you—not because I think you're lying, but because I need everyone else to see that we're being careful. That we're not stupid. You do exactly what we tell you when we tell you. No solo missions, no private communications, nothing off-book."

I paused.

"And if anything feels off—if you get a message, a dream, a *whisper*—you come to us immediately. Not an hour later. Not when it's convenient. Immediately. Understood?"

"Understood."

"And Zane?" I waited until he met my eyes. "If you're playing us—if any of this is an act—I will kill you myself. And I won't lose a minute's sleep over it. Clear?"

"Clear."

I nodded slowly. "Good. Welcome to the team."

He let out a breath that seemed to deflate him entirely, like a puppet with its strings cut. "Thank you," he whispered. "I know you don't have any reason to trust me. "

"Trust is earned," Eric said, putting a hand on his shoulder. The same gesture I'd seen him use with Allie a hundred times. "Telling us was a good first step."

Zane nodded, wiping his face with his sleeve. He looked exhausted, hollowed out, about ten years older than he had when he'd walked in. But there was something in his eyes that hadn't been there before. Something fragile but real.

Hope.

Allie moved then, crossing the room to stand beside him, not offering comfort exactly, but simply being *there.* A silent statement of...something. Solidarity, maybe. Or just the acknowledgment that they were both carrying things too heavy for anyone their age.

"Come on," she said quietly. "I'll walk you back to your room."

They left together, and I watched them go—two kids shaped by forces they never asked for, trying to figure out how to be something other than what they'd been made into.

Eddie waited until their footsteps had faded before he spoke. "You can't be serious."

I met his eyes. "I'm very serious."

"He's Samarek's son, Kate. That goddamn demon actually mated with a human, and he's the product. That just ain't good."

Eddie looked older than usual, the lines in his face deeper, his eyes sharp with worry. He'd been hunting demons longer than I'd been alive. His instincts had saved my life more than once.

But so had mine.

"He came to us," I said. "On his own. He could have run,

could have disappeared, could have kept playing whatever game his father set up—he asked to talk to us, and he told us everything."

"Or everything he wants you to believe."

"We just watched him break apart confessing it. I know what I saw, Eddie." I held up a hand before he could interrupt. "But I also know you're not wrong to be cautious. Keep watching him. Keep doubting. And keep second-guessing me. You know that's what I depend on you for."

Eddie snorted. "Fair enough, girlie. But if it goes sideways? If that kid turns out to be exactly what his daddy made him to be?"

"Then we deal with it. Together. The way we always have."

Eddie let out a breath that was half sigh, half growl. "Fine. But I'm watching him. Every move, every word, every time he so much as looks at one of those kids wrong. I'm watching."

"Good. That's exactly what I want."

He shook his head, muttering something about optimism being a luxury we couldn't afford, and shuffled out of the library, with Eric and me left standing alone in the silence he left behind.

"Do you think we're making a mistake?" I asked.

"Weren't you listening to me? You know I don't. That kid's been drowning his whole life, and we just threw him a rope. Whether he grabs it or pulls us under with him..." He shrugged. "That's the gamble we're taking."

"That about sums it up."

He looked at me, and something in his eyes made my breath catch. "Someone threw me a rope once, too. I grabbed it. Changed everything."

I knew he wasn't talking about Forza. Wasn't talking about demon hunting or training or even the demon that had been shoved inside him. He was talking about me. What I'd meant to him. And, I knew, what I still did.

"Get some rest," I said, because I didn't trust myself to say anything else. "Tomorrow's going to be a long day."

He nodded, and I watched him walk out of the library, and I thought about ropes and drowning and all the ways we save each other without meaning to.

20

KATE

*E*ddie followed me down the hall. "I'm still not sure," he said, his voice low. "But you're the headmistress. It's your call."

"Damn right it is," I said, making him grin.

"Careful girlie. I'll think you're starting to get a big head."

I grimaced. "Hardly. All I accomplished this morning was giving a lost boy some hope—and probably terrifying the students, too. I still have a portal that probably goes straight to hell in my basement."

He snorted. "Always the glass half-empty. You're starting to sound like me."

I paused, then tilted my head as I looked at him, that curmudgeonly face on a man who cared more than he wanted anyone to know. "Yeah, well, that wouldn't be a bad thing."

The tiniest, microscopic hint of a smile touched his lips. "See you at dinner."

"Deal," I said. "Unless that portal eats us first."

I heard his soft chuckle as he walked away...and hoped that my snappy comeback had been a joke and not a premonition.

I stood there for a moment, letting the silence settle. The

old mansion creaked around me, its bones shifting. Some-where upstairs, I could hear the muffled sounds of the students—voices, footsteps, the ordinary noises of young people trying to pretend their world hadn't just tilted sideways.

Something caught my eye, and I saw that Stuart was standing at the end of the hallway, near the stairs. He wasn't moving, wasn't calling out to me. Just standing there, watch-ing. When our eyes met, he raised one hand to gesture me over. I set off toward him, but the closer I got, the slower I wanted to move—and the tighter my chest became.

"Hey," I said.

"I heard about what you did in there. That was the right call for that boy."

"Is that the attorney or the oracle talking?"

"The father," he said. "So long as they can earn it, the saying's true."

"Saying?"

He shrugged. "Everyone deserves a second chance."

"I'm glad you think so."

He nodded. "I do. You deserve one as well. So do I."

I noted the fact that he didn't say that *we* deserved one. But all I said was, "What do you mean?"

He didn't answer at once, and as something in my chest went cold, I looked at him. Really looked at him. I'd watched this man for years. Playing with Timmy, hanging with Allie, helping me cook, which is something I need a lot of.

I'd watched him do yard work one day and give a campaign speech the next. I'd seen him put on a hard hat and dive into renovations on this incredible mansion.

And I'd seen him dead tired and scared, drained by visions, hollowed out by prophecies that ripped through him without warning or mercy. I'd seen him struggle to hold himself together when this world had met my old one, and nothing quite made sense for him anymore.

I'd seen all that and more. But I'd never seen him look like this. "What's wrong?"

"Nothing's wrong." He tried to smile. It didn't quite work. "Can we talk? Somewhere private?"

"Of course."

He led me upstairs to the large training room—empty now. Late afternoon light slanted through the high windows, painting everything gold and amber. It should have felt warm. But something about the tone in Stuart's voice made it feel like the light before a storm.

Stuart closed the door behind us, then pressed his forehead against it for a moment, his back to me, his shoulders rising and falling with a breath he seemed to be gathering from somewhere deep.

"Did you have a vision?"

He shook his head, then turned, and even though I'd looked into those eyes a million times, I couldn't read a thing in them.

"I'm leaving," he said.

The words didn't make sense at first. They just hung there in the air, disconnected from anything real.

"Leaving? Why?"

He shook his head. "I got a call from Rome the day of Allie's party. Do you remember?"

I nodded slowly, unsure where this conversation was going.

"It was Father Corletti. He suggested I come to Forza. Permanently. He wants me in Rome. To train with the oracles there, to learn how to control whatever this is that's happening to me," he said, pointing to his head.

"Oh." I stood looking at him, hating myself for not being sure how I felt.

"I'm going. Actually, I'm going tonight."

"Oh." A wave of grief crashed over me. Grief mixed with pain and loss and the slight stain of failure.

I opened my mouth to say something, realized I didn't know what, then closed it. I drew a breath and tried again. "And you're just telling me now?"

"I needed time to figure out what to say." He pushed off from the door and went to sit on a bench. "The visions aren't going to stop, Kate. They're exhausting. I need to learn how to deal with them."

"Well, yes. I get that. But..." I trailed off, hating myself for not saying what should come after *but*. That I loved him—I did. That Timmy needed him—true. That I wanted him to stay.

That one... Well, that one was the kicker, wasn't it?

I looked down at the floor. "I hate that this has happened to you."

"I don't," he said, and I jerked my head up in surprise.

"Really?"

"I've been an outsider in your life for years, jealous that you and Allie were able to do something so fundamentally important."

"Everything you've done—being an attorney, being a father, supporting the school, your visions. They're all important."

"Maybe. But that's not the only reason."

"Then what is? Because Timmy and I want to hear it."

He flinched, but to his credit he didn't falter. "Kate, please. You've seen what this has done to me. I can't be the father I should to Timmy. And I'm not what you need, either. Not anymore. Maybe not ever."

"That's not true."

"It is." His voice was gentle. Unbearably gentle. "And we both know it's not just the visions."

The room seemed to shrink. The golden light seemed to dim.

"Stuart."

"I know about you and Eric."

The words landed like a slap. I felt my face go hot, then cold. "No, Stuart, there's nothing going on with Eric."

He held up a hand. "I know it was just the one time. I think it might have been what pulled me out." He flashed a sideways grin as I tried not to melt into the floor. "Sorry about that," he said, with a tiny smile that somehow seemed both amused and sad.

"I'm sorry. I thought you were never going to wake up."

"And you love him." The words were simple, matter-of-fact.

"I love you, too," I said, hearing a note of panic in my voice.

"I know," he said. "The question is whether loving me is enough. Whether it's the same as what you feel for him." He squeezed my hands gently, then let go. "And we both know the answer to that."

I wanted to argue. Wanted to tell him he was wrong, that what we had mattered, that it was real and important and worth fighting for.

But the words wouldn't come. Because he wasn't wrong. He'd never been wrong about the things that mattered.

"I love you, Kate, I always will. You and Timmy and Allie." He drew a breath. "I see me, too. In the visions, I mean. Two paths. One staying here with you and the kids. One going to Rome. Learning. Doing something terribly important. Away from my family, yes. But knowing that you'd have each other. That you'd be as safe as you can considering the world you live in."

Tears streamed down my face.

"And Timmy?"

"I'll still see him." He grinned. "More than he'll see me if I learn to control this thing."

I actually laughed. "Won't that make his teenage years special?"

We shared a smile, and I sagged a little. "I get it," I said. "I'm so sorry, but I get it. I do love you."

He moved closer and took my hands in his. His fingers were warm. Familiar. How many times had I held these hands? How many years?

"I know you love me. That was never the question."

"I never wanted to hurt you," I whispered.

"I know that, too." He reached up, touched my cheek. The gesture was so tender it made my throat ache. "You held back as long as you could. I know what that cost you."

"It wasn't enough."

"It was more than most people would have given." He dropped his hand. Stepped back. "I'm not angry, Kate. I was, for a while. But then I realized—being angry at you for loving him is like being angry at the sun for rising. Some things just are. You can fight them, or you can accept them."

"And you're accepting?"

"I'm letting go and looking forward. You're the one who needs to think about acceptance."

"Oh," I said, not sure how to respond, or even what exactly he meant.

He pointed to his head. "I believe this happened for a reason. And I'm going to Rome. To figure out what it is."

I didn't know what to say. Didn't know how to let him go, this man who had been my anchor for so long. Who had stepped into my life when I was drowning in grief and given me something solid to hold onto.

"I've said goodbye to Timmy. I'm going to go talk to Allie, then go over the books with Laura. I have a car coming in a couple of hours to take me to the airport. Take care of yourself, Kate." He moved toward the door, then paused with his hand on the frame. "And ask Eric not to be smug in victory. It's not a good look for him." He tapped his head. "And that if he hurts you, I'll see it. And that I have a nasty right hook."

I laughed. Despite everything, I actually laughed.

"I love you," I said instead of goodbye.

"I know. I love you, too. Stay safe, Kate." He kissed my cheek, and then he was gone. And for a moment it was just me, alone in a house full of people.

21

ALLIE

Jared's chest was cool against my cheek, and I snuggled closer. We'd been lying like this for almost an hour, tangled together on my bed with the late afternoon light filtering through the curtains. His shirt was somewhere on the floor. I was down to my bra and leggings, which was as far as we ever went—not because I didn't want more, but because every time things started heading in that direction, one of us would pull back. Him, usually. Something about wanting to do this right.

It was simultaneously the most romantic and most frustrating thing anyone had ever done for me.

"It's right below us," I said, breaking the comfortable silence. "The portal. Like, down there underneath us all the time."

Jared's hand stilled on my back. "I try not to think about it."

"How can you not think about it? There's a door to hell in our basement. A door that's getting bigger. A door that my blood was supposed to close, except—" I pushed up on one elbow so I could see his face. "Why didn't it work? My blood closed the gates before. Why is this different?"

"I don't know." His dark eyes were troubled. "Different gate, I guess. Maybe the ritual has to be done with a chant. Or the moon has to be full. There's no way to guess."

"Maybe I'm not enough." The words came out smaller than I intended. "Maybe whatever Father Donnelly bred into me, whatever makes me special—it's not the right kind of special for this."

"Hey." Jared sat up, pulling me with him so we were facing each other. "You are more than enough. We just don't have all the pieces yet."

"What if we run out of time before we find them?"

He didn't answer. We both knew that was a real possibility.

I leaned into him, letting his arms wrap around me. "I keep thinking about what happens after," I admitted. "If we survive this. If we close the portal and beat Samarek and everything goes back to normal—whatever normal even means anymore."

"What about it?"

"Us. What happens to us." I pulled back enough to look at him. "You're immortal, Jared. Or close enough. And I'm going to get old and wrinkly and eventually die, and you're just going to—"

"Stop." His voice was firm but gentle. "We've talked about this."

"I know, but—"

"I don't care about forever. I care about now. I care about tomorrow. I care about as many days as we get, however many that turns out to be." He tucked a strand of hair behind my ear. "The rest, we figure out as we go."

I wanted to believe him. I really did. But the math never

worked out in my head, no matter how many times I tried to make it add up.

The door burst open.

"Allie, I need to talk to you about—oh my God! Sorry! Sorry! Sorry!" Mindy stood frozen in the doorway, eyes wide, face already turning red. Her gaze ping-ponged between Jared's bare chest and me in only my bra, and I could practically see her brain short-circuiting.

"Hey, Mom," I said, making Mindy cringe even more.

"I'm so sorry! I didn't—I should have knocked. I'll just—" She was already backing up, hands raised like she was surrendering.

"I really have to start locking that door," I said.

Jared, because he was Jared, was already reaching for his shirt. "It's fine. I can give you two some space."

"No, no, it's okay, I can come back, I'll just—" Mindy was fumbling for the door handle without looking at it. "Text me! Or don't! Whatever! Sorry!"

"Mindy." I grabbed a tee from the floor and tugged it on. "Calm down. It's fine. What's going on?"

She stopped retreating, but she still looked like she wanted the floor to swallow her. "It can wait. Seriously. I didn't mean to interrupt your...your..." She gestured vaguely at the bed.

"Our conversation?" I offered dryly.

"Sure. Yes. That."

Jared had his shirt back on now. He dropped a kiss on the top of my head. "I'll go take a cold shower."

I rolled my eyes as he squeezed my hand. "Text me later?"

I nodded, and he slipped past Mindy, who was still muttering apologies. She watched him go, then turned back to me with an expression that was part embarrassment, part adoration. It was the second part that made me melt.

"Okay," I said, patting the bed beside me. "Spill. What's the big deal?"

She hesitated, then crossed the room and perched on the edge of the mattress. "It's about Zane."

"What about him?"

"I don't think keeping him here is a good idea." The words came out in a rush. "I know your mom decided to trust him, and I know he confessed and everything, but Allie. He's Samarek's son. And I looked up Samarek. Like, really dug into the archives."

"And?"

"And he's insane. Like, genuinely, horrifically insane. The things he did to people. To himself. He literally replaced his own body parts with demon bits. And there are accounts of him keeping people alive for years while he experimented on them to learn how to do that." She shuddered. "Zane came from that monster. That's his father. That's his blood."

I felt something cold settle in my chest. "So you're scared of him because of something he had no choice in?"

"That's not what I'm saying."

"He didn't choose to be a demon's kid, Mindy. He didn't ask for any of this."

"I know that. But still."

"And he told my mom everything. He came forward on his own. He could have kept lying, but he didn't. He chose to tell the truth."

"Maybe." She had her stubborn face on. "People say what they need to say to survive. How do we know this isn't just another manipulation? Another move in whatever game Samarek's been playing?"

"Because I looked at his face when he talked about Trevor. Because I saw him fall apart. Because—"

"Because he seems like a nice guy, and that's all you can see. But what if that's a mask? He's right here living under the same roof with us."

Anger roared through me. "So we should just write people off because of where they came from? Because of what's in their blood?" I was on my feet now, the blanket falling away, too angry to care. "You know who else has demon stuff in their blood? My dad. You know who's an actual vampire? My boyfriend. The one you just walked in on and who didn't suck you dry for doing it. I mean, let's think. Oh, right, he was actually polite."

Mindy's face went pale. "That's not the same."

"How is it not the same? My dad carried a demon inside him for years. Jared is literally undead. And you're sitting here telling me we should be scared of Zane because his father is a monster?"

"I'm not saying that."

"Bullshit. You're saying exactly that." My hands were shaking. All the fear from the last few days, all the uncertainty about the portal and my blood and whether any of us were going to survive this—it was all pouring out now, aimed at the easiest target. "You're saying that blood is destiny. That what your parents did determines who you are. That people can't choose to be different."

"Allie, I'm just scared, okay?" Mindy's eyes were bright with tears. "I'm scared and I don't know what to do and I thought maybe you'd understand."

"Understand what? That my best friend thinks my dad and my boyfriend are ticking time bombs because of something they never chose?"

"That's not fair!"

"Get out."

Mindy stared at me. "Allie—"

"Get out." I grabbed the first thing my hand touched—a stuffed penguin Mindy had given me and that I love—and threw it at her. It bounced off her shoulder, harmless but pointed. "I can't talk to you right now. Just go."

She went. The door closed behind her with a soft click that somehow felt louder than a slam.

I stood there in the middle of my room, breathing hard, the anger draining out of me as quickly as it had come. In its place was something worse. Something that felt a lot like guilt.

Mindy was scared. We were all scared. And I'd just thrown her out for saying the quiet part out loud—the thing we were all thinking but nobody wanted to admit.

What if Zane was exactly what his father made him?

What if blood really was destiny?

What if the demon essence in my veins meant I was destined to become something terrible too?

I sank down onto the bed, pulled my knees to my chest, and tried very hard not to cry.

I don't know how long I sat there before the door opened again, soft and slow. Jared slipped inside, his hair still damp from the shower, and without a word he crossed to the bed and climbed in beside me. His arms wrapped around me, pulling me against his chest, and I let myself fold into him.

"You heard," I said. It wasn't a question.

"Stupid vampire hearing."

I laughed, but it was thin. Because as much as I didn't want to think it, I had the terrible feeling that my best friend was scared of me, and I didn't know what to do with that.

"She doesn't mean it," Jared said quietly. "She's just scared. We all are." His hand moved in slow circles on my back. "She loves you. And she must love me, too. I'm irresistible."

That almost got a real laugh out of me. Almost.

"If Zane's gone bad," Jared continued, his voice serious now, "it's because of his choices, not his parentage. You know that. Hell, so does Mindy." He pressed a kiss to my hair. "So don't you go forgetting it now."

I didn't say anything, just snuggled closer and silently hoped that Mindy remembered it, too.

22

KATE

I found Stuart in our bedroom—his bedroom now—packing the last of his things. The suitcase lay open on the bed, and he was folding shirts with the methodical precision of a man who'd learned to take care of himself long before I came along.

"Hey," I said from the doorway.

He looked up, and something in his face softened. "Hey yourself." He put down the shirt he'd been folding and sat on the edge of the bed. After a moment, he patted the space beside him. "I thought we already did the goodbye thing."

"We did. I just keep thinking I should feel worse about this," I finally admitted. "About us. About you leaving. And I do feel bad, Stuart. I feel terrible. But I also feel..." I trailed off, not sure how to finish.

"Relieved?" he offered quietly.

I closed my eyes. "That sounds awful. True, but awful."

"It sounds honest." His hand found mine, and he laced our fingers together the way he had a thousand times before. "Kate, look at me."

I did. His eyes were kind—they'd always been kind—and there was no accusation in them. No blame.

"I feel it, too," he said. "The relief. But here's what I've figured out—feeling relieved doesn't mean we failed. It just means we're being honest about where we ended up."

"When did you get so wise?"

He laughed softly. "Somewhere between the coma and the visions, I think. Near-death experiences have a way of clarifying things."

I leaned my head against his shoulder, and he let me. We sat like that for a while, two people who had loved each other, who still loved each other, but in a different way now.

"I don't regret it," I said. "Any of it. I need you to know that."

"I know."

"You gave me Timmy. You gave me years of normalcy. Of feeling like maybe I could have a regular life."

"You gave me a family. Not to mention this whole chaotic, demon-fighting, world-saving mess. And I loved it, Kate. I loved every minute of it."

"Even the parts where you almost died?"

"Even those." He squeezed my hand. "Though I could have done without the coma. As for the visions..." he trailed off with a shrug. "Those, I'm getting used to."

I laughed despite myself and felt tears prick at my eyes. "I'm going to miss you."

"I'm not dying. I'm going to Rome." He pulled back enough to look at me. "And I meant what I said. I'm not leaving Timmy's life. Video calls, visits, whatever it takes. He's my son. That doesn't change just because his parents couldn't make it work. That goes for Allie, too. I didn't suffer through that girl's puberty for nothing."

I laughed, wiping my eyes with my free hand. "I know you'll be there for him. For both of them."

Stuart was quiet for a moment. Then he stood, crossed to his dresser, and opened the top drawer. When he turned back, he was holding something small.

"I want you to have this."

It was a piece of paper, folded into quarters and soft with age. I took it carefully, unfolding it to reveal a child's drawing —stick figures in bright crayon, a house with a pointed roof, a yellow sun in the corner.

"Timmy's first drawing," Stuart said. "The one he made in preschool. 'My Family.' That's you, and that's supposed to be me, and that blob is either Allie or possibly a dog. He was three. Artistic accuracy wasn't his strong suit."

I remembered the day Timmy had brought this home, so proud of himself, demanding we put it on the refrigerator immediately. It had hung there for months before Stuart had quietly taken it down and—I'd assumed—thrown it away.

"You kept it."

"Of course I kept it." He sat back down beside me. "Kate, whatever else happens. Whatever choices we've both made. Whatever comes next. We made something good together. That little boy down the hall is the best thing I've ever done. And I wanted you to have something to remember that. To remember us before everything got complicated."

I looked at the drawing. At the crooked figures and the too-big sun. At the word FAMLY written across the top in wobbly letters.

"Thank you," I whispered. "For this. For everything."

Stuart leaned over and pressed a kiss to my forehead. It was gentle. Final.

"Be happy, Kate," he said. "You deserve it. And so does he."

I didn't have to ask who he meant.

I stood, still holding the drawing, and walked to the door. "Stuart?"

"Yeah?"

"For what it's worth, you were a good husband. A great father. And I'm sorry I couldn't be what you needed."

"You were exactly what I needed," he said. "For exactly as long as I needed it. That's not nothing, Kate. That's everything."

I nodded, not trusting my voice, and slipped out into the hallway.

Behind me, I heard him resume packing. Shirts folding. Drawers closing. The quiet sounds of a man preparing to leave.

I went to my room and tucked Timmy's drawing into my bedside table, next to the photo of Eric and me from our wedding day that I'd never quite been able to throw away.

Two lives. Two loves. Both real. Both true.

Soon, Stuart would leave for Rome.

And I would finally stop pretending I didn't know what I wanted.

THE EVENING HAD THAT GRAY, heavy quality that made everything feel muted. Like the world knew something was ending and had dressed appropriately.

The taxi sat in the circular driveway, its trunk already stuffed with Stuart's luggage. Not much, really—a few suitcases, a garment bag, a box of books he couldn't bear to leave behind. The rest he'd already planned to have us ship.

I stood on the front steps and watched him do a final check, patting his pockets for his passport, his phone, his wallet. The small rituals of departure.

We'd all gathered to see him off, clustering on the porch like mourners at a funeral no one wanted to admit was happening. Eddie stood with his arms crossed, his jaw working like he was chewing on words he couldn't quite spit out. Cutter and Laura flanked him, Laura already clutching a tablet, because she'd be taking over Stuart's administrative duties now.

The students had said their goodbyes earlier, most of them awkward and uncertain. Stuart had never been their teacher, just a steady presence in the mansion. The oracle who saw too much and said too little. The quiet man who sometimes screamed in his sleep when the visions took him. They didn't know what to make of his leaving.

Neither did I.

A breeze picked up, carrying the smell of the ocean and something else—rain coming, maybe, or just the particular scent of change. I wrapped my arms around myself even though I wasn't cold.

Allie broke from the group first. She crossed the gravel drive in quick strides and wrapped her arms around Stuart in a fierce hug, the kind that said everything words couldn't. I watched his face over her shoulder—the way his eyes closed, and his arms tightened around her. The way he seemed to be memorizing the moment.

"I love you," I heard her say, her voice muffled against his shoulder. "You know that, right? No matter what happens, no matter how far away you are. I love you."

"I know." He hugged her back just as fiercely. "I love you, too, kiddo. I'll be seeing you a lot. We'll make Forza charter a plane. You train. We hang out. Sound good?"

"Perfect."

"Take care of your mom for me."

She nodded. "Always."

When she pulled away, her eyes were bright with tears. She retreated to Jared's side, and he put an arm around her shoulders, steady and sure. She leaned into him like he was the only thing keeping her upright.

Stuart turned to Timmy, who had been clinging to my leg with the particular intensity of a child who sensed something was wrong but didn't understand what. "Hey, buddy. Come here."

Timmy let go of me and toddled over, his dinosaur sneakers scuffing against the gravel. Stuart scooped him up, holding him close, pressing his face into Timmy's hair for a long moment. I saw his shoulders shake once—just once—before he got control of himself.

Timmy, being Timmy, tolerated the affection for about three seconds before squirming. "Down! Wanna play with Elena!"

Stuart laughed a real laugh, the first I'd heard from him in days. It cracked something open in my chest. "Okay, okay." He set Timmy down and watched him race across the lawn toward where Fran and Elena were waiting near the garden. "He's going to be fine," Stuart said, almost to himself. "He won't even remember this by lunchtime."

"He's resilient."

"He is." Stuart's eyes stayed on our son for another moment. "Make sure he knows I love him."

"I will. And you can tell him yourself everytime you talk on the phone. And we'll be visiting at least twice a year. Who worries about the cost of international travel when *Forza*'s paying the airfare?"

Eric stepped forward then, and I realized I was hugging myself. The two men faced each other—my past and my present, my first love and my second.

And my first again.

Eric extended his hand, and Stuart took it.

Their grips held for a beat longer than necessary. "Take care of her," Stuart said. "Of them."

Eric nodded. "I will. I promise."

I saw Stuart's face change. The tension in his jaw softened. Something that might have been gratitude flickered in his eyes.

Stuart nodded as he released Eric's hand. Then he was turning away, climbing into the taxi, the door closing behind him with a sound that felt far too final. The engine started, and I watched it roll down the long drive, finally disappearing around the bend where the oak trees blocked the view.

I kept watching even after it was gone. Kept listening even after the sound of the engine faded into nothing. Kept standing there on the steps while the others drifted away one by one, back into the house, back to their duties and their distractions and their carefully maintained illusions of normalcy.

"Kate?"

I turned. Laura stood a few feet away, the tablet still clutched to her chest like armor. She looked tired—we all looked tired these days—but there was something else in her expression. Sympathy, maybe. Or just the particular exhaustion of being the one who kept everything running while everyone else fell apart.

"Father Corletti's on the phone," she said. "He says it's important."

"Of course it is." I managed a small smile. "Everything's important these days."

"I can take a message if you need a minute."

"No." I straightened my shoulders. Pushed the grief—or whatever it was—down into the place where I kept all the things I couldn't afford to feel. "I'll take it. Which line?"

"Stuart's office. I transferred it there."

I hurried inside, not surprised to find that the office still smelled like him. I sat in his chair, and grabbed up the phone, longing for Father's voice.

"Father."

"Ah, Katherine." His voice crackled through the line, the connection from Rome never quite as clear as it should be in the age of fiber optics. There was warmth in it, though. There always was. Father Corletti had been more of a father to me than anyone else in my life, and even across an ocean, I could feel his presence like a steadying hand. "I trust Stuart is safely on his way?"

"Just left. He'll see you soon."

"Good. Good." He cleared his throat. "I had hoped to send Father Donnelly to assist you with the Samarek situation. Unfortunately, an urgent matter has arisen here that requires his attention. He will not be able to come."

I let out a breath I hadn't realized I'd been holding. My shoulders dropped. Something tight in my chest loosened.

"That's really not a problem. I mean, the more the merrier for fighting, but, well, you know."

"Because you do not trust him."

There was no point in pretending. "Eliza does. And I know he and I are related. But you said it. I really don't. Especially not after learning what he did to Eric. To Allie. All those experiments, Father. All that breeding program nonsense. He played God with their lives. With my family's lives. He put demon bits into a child and called it science, called it necessary, called it serving a higher purpose. So not sorry he can't come."

"I understand. Much of life is complicated. There are many facets. And your instincts have always served you well. I would not ask you to ignore them now."

There was a pause, and I heard him take a sip of what I knew would be tea. "Tell me, child, what do you know of Samarek's current state?"

We talked for a while about the portal, about what we'd found in the basement, about Trevor's body and the blood and the failed attempt with Allie's blood that should have worked but didn't. Father listened more than he spoke, asking the occasional question, making small sounds of acknowledgment. I could picture him in his study in Rome, surrounded by his books and his crosses and his centuries of accumulated wisdom, processing everything I told him and filing it away in that vast, orderly mind.

"We're trying to figure out Stuart's prophecy, but we don't have a good idea yet. Allie's blood was our best guess, but obviously that didn't work. Maybe Stuart will remember something that was in his head but that he didn't speak."

I hoped so. The vessel of light that's shadowed? Allie had been sure that was referring to her blood. Someone with a soul but tainted. But since that didn't work, there had to be another interpretation.

"We shall all keep pondering," Father said. "And you must take care. All of you," he said.

"We will. Eric and Laura have been going through the archives with Mindy and Zane, looking for anything about Samarek's methods. So far, nothing useful." I paused. "About Zane," I began, then wasn't sure how to continue. I'd written everything up and sent Father an email, but this was the first time we'd spoken.

"You did the right thing," he assured me. "That boy is a victim, too. Not as much as Trevor, but we do not try to count pain. That is never wise. Let him help, Katherine. It would do his soul good to help undo some of what he helped his father wreak."

"We will," I promised.

The conversation shifted then, the way it always did when I spoke with Father. "And how are you, Katherine? Truly?"

I leaned back in Stuart's chair. "I don't know," I admitted. "Relieved that Stuart's going somewhere he can get help. Sad that he's gone." I swallowed against the tightness in my throat. "And guilty that the sadness isn't...bigger. Does that make sense?"

"It makes perfect sense."

"I feel like I should be devastated. He's my husband. He's the father of my son. He's leaving because of me, because I—" I stopped. Started again, "You remember what happened, right? When Stuart was in the coma. When we thought he might never wake up. Eric and I..."

"I remember." His voice held no judgment. It never did. "You confessed this to me some time ago, if you recall."

"Yes."

He had given me absolution, but I'd had to find a way to carry it myself . "I still feel terrible about it. And now this. The visions. It's a lot.

"It is. But Katherine. That is not your fault. You did not cause his suffering. You did not choose for him to become an oracle."

"I know.

"You have done much good in this world." His voice was firm now, the voice of the priest who had trained me, who had believed in me when I didn't believe in myself. "You have saved lives. Protected innocents. Raised a remarkable daughter. You have earned the right to happiness."

He paused, and when he spoke again, his tone was softer. Almost teasing. "And when that which makes you most happy is practically offered up on a silver platter, perhaps you should not run from it. Perhaps you should embrace it."

I couldn't help it. I smiled. Actually smiled, for the first time all day. "You always see too much, Father."

"It is both my gift and my curse." I could hear the warmth in his voice, the affection that had sustained me through so many dark nights.

"Stuart will be an asset here in Rome. The oracles are eager to work with him, to help him understand and control his abilities. And he will still be in touch with his son. This is not an ending, Katherine. It is a transition. A door closing so that another may open."

"I hope you're right."

"I am old and occasionally wise. Trust me in this, if nothing else."

When I hung up, the office was quiet around me. Stuart's books still lined the shelves. His handwriting still covered the calendar. His absence still filled every corner of the room.

But something had shifted. Some weight I'd been carrying without realizing it had lifted, just slightly. Just enough to breathe.

My eyes drifted to the corkboard on the wall above the desk. Stuart had pinned various things there over the months —schedules, notes, reminders, a few photographs. But tucked in the corner, almost hidden behind a flyer was something else.

A drawing. Small. Crayon on construction paper.

I stood and crossed to the board, pulling the paper free.

Red door. Gold doorknobs. The same image Timmy had been drawing for weeks now, over and over, scattered around the house like warnings I'd been too busy to read. But this one was different.

This one had the shadow.

Behind the door, pressing against the frame like something trying to get out, was a dark shape. Darker than the other shadows Timmy drew. More defined. More deliberate. It had eyes, two small circles, carefully filled in with black crayon. And it was looking at something.

A small figure stood in front of the door. A stick figure with yellow hair and blue dots for eyes.

A little boy.

Standing right in front of the thing that was trying to get through.

The knocking man is happy today, Mommy.

Timmy's voice echoed in my head, casual and unconcerned, the way kids are when they don't understand that the things they're saying should be terrifying.

He's happy. He was knocking really loud last night.

I'd asked him about it that morning, crouched down to his level in the kitchen while he fidgeted and asked for pancakes. He'd shrugged like it was nothing. Like everyone heard knocking from behind doors that shouldn't exist.

I stared at the drawing. At the shadow with its careful crayon eyes. At the little boy standing between it and the world.

My son. My baby. Drawing pictures of the thing in our basement.

I was out of the office and halfway up the stairs before I even realized I was moving, the drawing still clutched in my hand, Timmy's name on my lips like a prayer.

I found him in the playroom with Elena, the two of them building a lopsided tower out of wooden blocks. Fran sat nearby with a book, glancing up when I burst through the door.

"Kate? Is everything okay?"

"Fine." The word came out too fast, too breathless. "Everything's fine. I just wanted to check on him."

Timmy looked up at me with a smile. "Mommy! Look what we builded!"

"Built," I corrected automatically, crossing the room to kneel beside him. "It's beautiful, baby."

"It's a castle. For the dinosaurs."

"Of course it is."

I pulled him into my arms, hugging him tighter than I should have, breathing in the little-boy smell of him—grass and sunshine and the grape juice he'd had at snack time. He tolerated it for about three seconds before squirming.

"Mommy, you're squishing me!"

"Sorry." I let him go, then watched him turn back to his blocks like nothing had happened. Like he hadn't been drawing pictures of the monster in our basement. Like he hadn't been hearing it knock.

I stayed there for a long moment, crouched on the play-room floor, the drawing crumpled in my fist. My son was fine. Happy. Building castles for dinosaurs with his best friend.

And somewhere beneath us, the thing behind the red door was getting stronger.

The knocking man was happy.

I smoothed out the drawing, looked at those careful crayon eyes one more time, and tried very hard not to scream.

23

ALLIE

The house felt wrong without Stuart in it. He was my father as much as Daddy was. More in some ways. While Daddy was off being dead, Stuart had been the one who'd shown up for school plays and argued with me about curfews and suffered through my most obnoxious teenage years.

And now he was on a plane to Rome, and the house felt emptier. Quieter. Like someone had turned down the volume on everything.

I found Jared in the common room, sprawled on one of the old leather couches with a book he wasn't reading. Zane sat in the window seat on the far side of the room, as far from everyone else as he could get without actually leaving. He had a book too. Neither of them was turning pages.

"Hey," Jared said, looking up as I dropped onto the couch beside him. "How are you holding up?"

"I'm fine." He just looked at me. "Okay, I'm not fine. Stuart just left for Rome, Trevor is dead, there's a literal doorway to hell in our basement, and—" I stopped. Swallowed. "And I threw a stuffed penguin at my best friend's head and told her to get out of my room."

"The penguin thing does seem like a low point."

"It was Mr. Penguin. She gave him to me." I pulled my knees up to my chest and wrapped my arms around them. Outside, the sky was the color of old dishwater. It had been gray for days now, like even the weather knew something terrible was coming.

Zane hadn't moved from the window seat. He was watching us, I realized. Not in a creepy way—more like a kid at a new school, trying to figure out where he fit. Or if he fit at all.

The door creaked open, and Mindy stood in the doorway, her eyes red-rimmed, her shoulders hunched like she was bracing for a blow. She looked like she'd been crying for hours. She looked the way I felt. "Can I come in?" Her voice was barely above a whisper.

Part of me wanted to say no. Part of me was still angry—at the things she'd said, at the way she'd looked at me like I was something to be afraid of.

But a bigger part of me was just tired. Tired of fighting. Tired of being scared. Tired of everything. "Yeah," I said. "Come in." She crossed the room slowly, like she was approaching a wild animal, then stopped a few feet away from the couch, her hands twisting together. "I'm sorry," she said, apparently not caring that Jared and Zane were there, both with their heads down as if they were trying to be invisible.

"About what I said," Mindy added. "I didn't mean it. Not really. I was scared, and I let the fear make me stupid, and I'm sorry."

I didn't say anything.

"I've known Jared for years," Mindy continued, glancing at him. "I never once thought of him—you—as a monster. And your dad is literally one of the best people I've ever met, even with everything he's been through. I know that. I know the demon stuff doesn't make you evil. I just—"

She hiccupped, tears spilling over. "I read about Samarek. About what he's done. The experiments, the manipulations, the way he twists people. And I got so scared that I forgot who my friends actually are."

"It hurt," I said quietly. "What you said. It really hurt."

"I know. I'm so sorry."

"I'm not a monster, Mindy."

"I know you're not. I've always known that." We stood there, looking at each other across a distance that felt much wider than the few feet of carpet between us. I thought about all the years of friendship. All the secrets we'd shared. All the times she'd had my back, and I'd had hers. One fight didn't erase all of that. Even a bad one.

"I shouldn't have thrown Mr. Penguin at you," I said finally.

She laughed—a wet, choked sound. "I deserved it."

"Maybe. But he didn't."

That got a real laugh out of her, wobbly but genuine. I felt something loosen in my chest. Not forgiveness, exactly. But the beginning of it. The possibility. "Come here," I said, and opened my arms. She practically fell into the hug, holding on tight, and I held on too. My best friend. My sister in everything but blood.

When we finally pulled apart, both of us were crying. The good kind of crying, though.

Jared was watching us with a soft expression. "Better?" he whispered.

"Getting there," Mindy said, making me laugh.

Zane hadn't moved from the window seat. He was looking out at the gray sky now, giving us privacy, or maybe just uncomfortable with the emotional display.

I couldn't blame him. He'd confessed to being Samarek's

son. To marking Trevor. The fact that he was still in this house at all was a testament to my mom's willingness to take risks. Or her desperation. Hard to tell which.

"Zane," I said.

He turned, wary. "Yeah?"

"You don't have to sit over there like you're in quarantine."

He didn't move. "I kind of feel like I should be."

"My mom said you're part of the team now."

"Provisionally," he said.

I shrugged. "That's more than a lot of people get."

He was quiet for a long moment. "I keep thinking about Trevor." He stopped. Swallowed hard. "He trusted me. I was the closest thing he had to a friend here, and I used that. I used him."

"Did you know?" Mindy asked. Her voice was careful, neutral. "Did you know what would happen?"

"No." The word came out fierce, almost angry. "I swear I didn't. I thought it was just...tracking. Or protection. Something harmless. I didn't know it was a death sentence."

"But you did it without asking questions."

Zane flinched. "Yeah. I did. He was my dad. I trusted him. But I shouldn't have." The room went quiet. I could hear the old house creaking around us, settling into its bones. Somewhere downstairs, the portal was pulsing, hungry, waiting to be fed.

"I've done things without asking questions, too," Jared said quietly. "When I was younger. When I was still figuring out what I was." He looked at Zane steadily. "It doesn't make it okay. But it makes it understandable."

"Understandable isn't the same as forgivable," Zane said.

"No. It's not." Jared shifted on the couch. "But forgivable isn't the same as impossible, either."

Zane looked at him for a long moment, then nodded

slowly. "Yeah. I get that. And I want to help. I know you don't trust me. I know I haven't earned it. But I want to help close that portal. I want to stop him."

"Then help." I pulled out my phone, checking the time. "Mom said we're meeting in the library in an hour to go over what we know."

Mindy stood. "I need to go do some more research," she said, then looked at me. "We're good?"

I nodded. "We're good," I said. We both grinned, and then she hurried from the room.

The door closed behind her. Jared stretched. "I should go check in with your mom. She's been staring at one of Timmy's drawings all morning. The one with the shadow behind the door."

My stomach tightened. "The Knocking Man."

Jared nodded, his face grim. "She's trying to figure out what Timmy's seeing. Whether it's prophecy or just kid stuff."

"It's not kid stuff."

"No. It's not." He stood, then bent to press a kiss to my forehead. "Back in a bit," he said, then headed out, leaving me alone with Zane, a boy I wanted to trust, but wasn't quite there.

I hoped I was wrong. I hoped when it came down to it, he'd be on our side and not his father's.

I hoped for the sake of his soul. And also because despite everything, he was a friend. And I really didn't want to have to take him down.

24

KATE

Laura found me in the kitchen that evening, staring at a glass of wine I hadn't touched.

"That bad?" She slid onto the stool beside me and reached for the bottle. "Or are you saving it for a special occasion?"

"I don't know what I'm doing."

"With the wine or with life in general?"

"Yes."

She poured herself a glass, then topped off mine even though it was still full. "How are you holding up?"

"I don't know that either." I finally picked up my glass, swirled the wine without drinking it. "I should be devastated, right? My husband just moved to another continent. And I'm sitting here feeling..." I searched for the word. "Lighter. Like I've been holding my breath for months and I finally get to exhale."

"That's not a crime, Kate. Especially not with all you two have been through. First husband back from the dead. Current husband having freakish visions. Neither crime nor misdemeanor."

I almost smiled but didn't. "It feels like one."

Laura set her glass down and studied me. She had that look—the one she got before lecturing Mindy.

"Okay," I said. "Lay it on me."

She rolled her eyes. "I was just going to say that you loved Stuart. You still love Stuart. But with that whole oracle thing, you've been in limbo for over a year now—longer, really, if we're counting from when Eric came back."

I shifted uncomfortably. Because yeah. We definitely had to count from when Eric came back.

"You've been trying to be a good wife to a man who was turning into someone neither of you recognized, while the love of your life was sleeping under the same roof." She raised an eyebrow. "That's exhausting. Feeling relief doesn't make you a bad person. It makes you human."

"When did you get so wise?"

"I've always been wise. You just don't listen."

"You know me so well," I said, and we both laughed.

A moment passed. Then another. And another. Finally, I said, "He knows. About me and Eric. That one time. The visions showed him."

"Ouch. How'd he take it?"

"Better than I deserved." I drew in a breath, remembering. "He said being angry at me for loving Eric was like being angry at the sun for rising."

"That's either incredibly generous or incredibly passive-aggressive."

"It was generous. That's what makes it worse."

We sat in silence for a moment. Somewhere in the house, I could hear the muffled sounds of the students—laughter, footsteps, the ordinary noises of young people who—even though they'd been warned—still had no concept of how close they were to something terrible.

"So," Laura said finally. "What now?"

I flashed a *well, duh* look at her. "I figured we'd try to close the portal and bind Samarek."

"Well, yeah, sure. Because there's always a demon to destroy. I meant now that Stuart's gone. About Eric. The thing that was holding you back isn't holding you back anymore."

I shrugged. I'd been asking myself the same question since Stuart's taxi disappeared around the bend. "I don't know."

"Bullshit."

"Laura—"

"You know exactly what you want. You've known for months. Years, probably." She leaned forward. "The question isn't what you want. The question is whether you're going to let yourself have it."

"It's not that simple."

"It's exactly that simple." She ticked off points on her fingers. "Eric loves you. Has always loved you. He would walk through hellfire for you—has, in fact, literally done that. You love him. Stuart has released you. The only thing standing between you and the thing you want is you."

"I know," I admitted. "But I worry. He's done some stupid, reckless shit."

"I have a feeling he was sometimes stupid and reckless back when you were together before."

She wasn't wrong. "What if it doesn't work out?" Because, yeah, that was my big fear. What if the thing I'd been wanting ever since I knew Eric was back turned out to be a McGuffin? "What if we try and it falls apart and we lose everything?"

"What if you don't try and you spend the rest of your life wondering?"

"I hate it when you decide to be wise."

"Yeah. I'm annoying that way." She reached over to squeeze my hand. "Look. I get it. It's scary. After everything you've been through—losing him the first time, building a life with Stuart, losing Stuart to the visions, getting Eric back but not really having him—the idea of actually being together, for real, with nothing in the way? That's got to be a little terrifying."

"It is."

She took a long sip of wine before continuing. "But nothing's going to happen if you don't make it happen. Men are idiots. Even the good ones. Especially the good ones. They'll wait forever, convinced they're being noble, while you're over here waiting for them to make a move."

"Voice of experience?"

"How do you think I ended up with Cutter?" She laughed. "That man would have pined from a distance for the next decade if I hadn't grabbed him by the collar and told him we were doing this."

"And how did that work out?"

"The results were awesome." Her smile turned wicked. "Very, very awesome."

"I didn't need to know that."

"Yes you did. Because here's the thing—you're not going into this blind. Eric already loves you. You already love him. You've already been married, had a daughter together, faced death together. This isn't a risk. This is a sure thing that you're too scared to claim."

I stared at my wine and thought about the woman holding the glass. The woman—who'd faced demons and portals and ancient evil but couldn't seem to walk down a hallway and knock on a door.

"Stuart left partly so I could be with him," I admitted quietly. "He told me that. He said he was letting me go so I could be a family with Eric."

"Then don't waste the gift he gave you." Laura stood, taking her wine with her. "Stuart loved you enough to leave. The least you can do is love yourself enough to stay."

She left me alone in the kitchen with a full glass of wine and an empty list of excuses.

I sat there for a long time, thinking about doors. The one in our basement that led to hell. The one Stuart had walked through this morning. The one three doors down from my bedroom that I'd been too afraid to knock on.

Some doors, once opened, changed everything.

Maybe it was time to stop being afraid of that.

Maybe.

I hadn't decided yet. But at least I'd decided to decide.

Timmy's room smelled like baby shampoo and the lavender sachets Fran tucked into his dresser drawers. I stood in the doorway for a moment, watching him arrange Boo Bear against his pillow with the kind of intense concentration only small children can muster.

"Mommy." He looked up, and his whole face brightened. "You came."

"Of course I came." I crossed to his bed and sat on the edge, brushing the hair back from his forehead. It needed cutting again. It always needed cutting. "Did you think I wouldn't?"

"Fran said you were busy."

"Never too busy for you, baby."

He scooted over to make room, and I stretched out beside him, Boo Bear wedged between us. The ceiling above his bed had glow-in-the-dark stars that Stuart had put up when we'd first moved into the mansion. Back when everything had felt like a fresh start.

"Mommy?"

"Hmm?"

"Is the house sick?"

I turned my head to look at him. His eyes were wide and serious in the dim glow of his nightlight. "What do you mean, sweetheart?"

"It feels wrong." He clutched Boo Bear tighter. "Like when my tummy hurts but I can't find where."

My chest constricted, terrified that my little boy was tuned in to this horror.

"The house is fine," I said, and the lie tasted sour on my tongue. "It's old, that's all. Old houses make funny noises."

"It's not the noises." He was quiet for a moment, his small fingers working at Boo Bear's matted fur. "It's the Knocking Man. He's louder now."

The room seemed to get colder. *Louder?* That had to mean the portal was getting stronger.

"He's still knocking?" I kept my voice light, casual, even as my heart hammered against my ribs.

Timmy nodded. "He wants to come in. He's been knocking for a long time. But the door's locked." He yawned, his eyelids drooping. "He says the lock is almost broken."

Almost broken.

Ice cold fear cut through me.

How much time did we actually have?

"Timmy." My voice came out steadier than I expected. "Has the knocking man talked to you? More than before?"

"No, Mommy." His eyes were closing now, sleep pulling him under despite the horror show playing out in my head. "But he thinks louder now."

I shivered. "What does he think about?"

"Coming home." Timmy's voice was barely a whisper now. "He wants to come home. And he thinks about the girl. The one with the bright light inside."

Allie. That must mean Allie.

My blood turned to ice.

"But mostly he thinks about me now," Timmy continued,

and my heart stopped entirely. "He says I'm special. He says not all little boys can talk to him."

"Timmy, listen to me." I pulled him closer, probably too tightly, but I didn't care. "Don't talk to the knocking man. Don't listen to him. If you hear him thinking, you think about something else. Boo Bear or Elena or dinosaurs or anything else. Okay?"

"But he likes me."

"And this is a fun game he likes, too. So promise me. Promise you'll play this game?"

"Okay, Mommy," he said, unaware that something ancient and terrible was trying to use him as a doorway.

"I told him no anyway," Timmy added, nestling into my arms. "I told him you wouldn't let him in. I said my mommy fights monsters."

I forced myself not to gasp, then held him tight, letting him drift to sleep as I stared at the glow-in-the-dark stars on the ceiling and felt the cold weight of fear settle into my bones.

This wasn't just a portal anymore. This wasn't just Samarek trying to get to Allie.

He was targeting my son.

We'd been focused on closing the portal. On researching and training and preparing.

But now we were out of time for all of that. This thing was stalking my boy, and we needed to end it now.

I pressed my lips to Timmy's forehead, breathing in the little-boy smell of him, the shampoo and the warmth and the absolute trust. He believed I could protect him. Believed it without question or doubt.

I had to make that true.

And so I eased myself out of his bed, tucking the covers around him, positioning Boo Bear within easy reach. At the door, I paused and looked back at his small form in the night-light glow.

"I won't let him in," I said, a promise carved from steel and terror and a mother's love. "I swear I will keep you safe."

As I whispered, Timmy slept on, peaceful and trusting.

And somewhere below us, in the dark beneath the bones of saints, something ancient kept knocking. Louder now. Almost through.

I needed to find Eric. We needed to close that portal.

And we needed to do it tonight.

I'D KNOWN I would find him in the library. That was where he always retreated when he needed to think or relax or puzzle something out. That was one of the things I loved most about him—the way he puzzled things out instead of leaping straight into the fray as I always had. And that was part of why he'd loved me—because we'd each fit each other's open spaces, the last piece in a jigsaw puzzle.

We always had. And, I knew, we still did.

He looked up when I came in and flashed that familiar smile. Tonight, though, it didn't quite reach his eyes.

"He's knocking at the door," I said, then tasted tears and realized I was crying. Immediately, Eric was at my side, his fingers twining with mine.

"Tell me," he said.

"Timmy." It was all I could manage. I had to force the sobs back before saying more. "The Knocking Man from before. Oh, God, Eric, he's Samarek, and he's going to try to hurt my little boy."

"He won't." He tilted my chin up so that I was looking straight at him. "We won't let him. Kate," he whispered. "We're going to end this."

I started to nod, but he cupped his hands to my face, then pressed his forehead against mine. He leaned in, and even through all my emotional chaos and fear, I wanted his kiss, his touch, and when his lips closed over mine, it was all I could do not to pull him down to the floor and lose myself in touch and memory and a wild, untamed longing.

That didn't happen.

Instead, we leaped apart, startled by the way the door slammed open and Mindy cried out, "Aunt Kate! Oh! I, um, it's opening! The portal is opening. Like, right now."

That cut through everything, and just like that we were racing through the hall joined by Zane and Ren and Ana.

"Just now. We heard a rumble and went to look. Jared and Allie did the recon—they're the fastest. But we didn't even need them to get close. Not really. We could see its glow from all the way across the basement."

She paused for a breath. "Marcus is already heading down with Eliza and Cutter and Sophie. It's not just Samarek they're fighting. It's demons, too. I don't know how they got down there. But there's like a dozen of them."

"Well, hell," Eric said. "There must be a hidden tunnel."

He was probably right. Which meant that more corporeal demons would be joining the party—a guess that immediately proved to be right when I heard them rampaging through the mansion.

"Keep us busy up here so that they can do what they do down there," Eric said, and he wasn't wrong.

"Anyone not already in the basement, get armed and get fighting. Eric and I are going down. And trigger the house alarm. Get the staff and Timmy and Elena in one place—not the Safe Room. The battle will be right under it. Outside in the parking lot would be best. Close to the street. Lots of eyes." I swallowed. "Keep them safe, Mindy," I said, wishing I had time to run to Timmy. To see his sweet face.

But there would be time enough after. I was going to make sure of that.

With a firm nod, Mindy darted out of the room, Eric and I rushing right out behind her but heading in the opposite direction. Not to outside and safety, but to the portal and the battle. And the place where were going to finally take Samarek down.

ALLIE

The house had become a war zone.

I had fought zillions of demons, but I'd never seen anything like this—dozens of them pouring through the hallways, crashing through windows, tearing through the place that had become my home.

They were in human bodies, mostly, but some had come in their true form and were skittering around, joints bending in ways joints aren't meant to bend, sharp teeth bared. Cold, flat eyes.

"Allie, down!"

I hit the floor as Jared's blade sang over my head, taking out a demon that had been lunging for my back. I whipped around and finished it off with a jab through the eye, releasing the demon that had invaded the body back to the ether.

"The portal," I gasped, scrambling to my feet. "We have to get to the portal."

"Kind of busy here!"

He wasn't wrong. The first floor had become a battle-ground—Marcus with his twin short swords, carving through demons with the brutal efficiency of someone who'd been doing this for decades. Cutter back-to-back with Aunt Laura, who hardly ever fought, but was doing a solid job.

Eddie was in the midst of it, too, way more spry than he should be for his age, and he was darting through the fray, tossing holy water vials like grenades.

As for the students, they were holding their own, and I was pretty damn proud.

"Allie!"

I turned to see Mom rush into the room, a knife in one hand and Timmy clutched against her hip with the other. He was crying—not the screaming terror I'd expected, but quiet, hiccupping sobs, his face buried against her shoulder.

"Status?"

"They're not trying to hold ground," Marcus said. "They're buying time."

"For Samarek."

"Has to be."

Mom's jaw tightened. She scanned the room, and I saw the moment she made a decision.

"Zane."

Eliza covered him as he turned toward Mom. "Yeah?"

"I need you to take Timmy, Mrs. Micari, and Mindy. Get them out of here. Take the back stairs, go through the garden, get to Eddie's shop downtown. Mindy knows where it is. Don't stop for anything."

"No," I said, rushing to join them. "Samarek's down there. We may need Zane here."

She nodded. "You're right," she said, then called Ren, Mindy, and Ana over. She gave them the same instructions, then sent them hurrying off, swearing they'd keep Timmy safe.

Zane's face went carefully blank. "You don't trust me. That's why you wanted me gone."

"If I didn't trust you, I wouldn't have tried to entrust my son to you. But Allie's right. We need you here. You, too," she said, looking at me. To Jared, she said. "I need you in charge here. Keep them safe."

"Yes, Ma'am," he said, and she grinned, then looked at me and the others.

She turned to Zane. "Let's go."

Something shifted in Zane's face, and he nodded. "I've got your back."

Mom smiled. "I know."

"Fran and Elena?" he asked.

I saw it on Mom's face—the surprise and respect at his concern.

"I sent them away last night. They're at Disneyland by now. Come on," Mom said as she turned back toward the chaos, her face hardening into something I recognized—a Hunter. A woman who had been fighting demons since before I was born. And I was weirdly, awesomely proud to be her kid.

"Allie, Zane," she said "With me. Jared, stay here and keep them away from us.

"On it," he said.

"Where?" I asked.

"The basement." She checked her knife, grabbed a second one from the weapons rack by the door. "Whatever's coming through that portal, we end it tonight."

Daddy slid in to join us, and we moved toward the basement, the battle raging on behind us as we hurried forward toward the ancient and terrible thing that was clawing its way into our world.

I gripped my stiletto tighter and followed my parents into the dark.

26

ALLIE

The basement had turned into a literal nightmare.

The portal had grown; the gaps between the "door" and its "frame" were wider now, and I wondered what had fed it. Not blood—not unless some innocent had been secretly brought in and sacrificed. I shivered at the thought.

No, more likely it had been feeding off fear. Either way, the gaps were wide, the door ready to swing open unencumbered.

I peered down into the oily darkness of the gap and drew in a sharp breath when I saw that something—someone—was down there beneath the disgusting membrane that had grown in the space.

The Knocking Man, massive and dark, pressing against the barrier between worlds. Not human. Not even close to human. Something ancient and terrible that had been waiting for this moment for a very, very long time.

"Samarek," Dad whispered.

The demon moved. Pressed harder. And then a hand emerged, fingers too long, the joints bending in directions they shouldn't, the skin the color of dried blood.

"My bride."

The rough, cruel voice came from everywhere and nowhere, reverberating around us. "At last."

It was looking at me.

"What the hell is it talking about?" I stumbled backward, bumping into Mom who looked as horrified as I felt.

"That bastard," she whispered, and I knew she didn't mean the demon.

That's when I understood. The way Father Donnelly had put a demon inside Daddy. The way I inherited that essence. He hadn't just been trying to create a super-Hunter, he'd been trying to create a bride for this monster. *The collar hides the teeth.*

Stuart's prophecy was right.

"You." The hand reached further through, followed by an arm, a shoulder. The portal stretched around it like a wound tearing open. "You were made for me. Bred for me. Blood and essence and power, crafted across generations. My perfect vessel. My bride."

It had never been about saving the world.

It was about creating something Samarek could use.

"I was the endgame," I whispered. "This whole time. I was Donnelly's endgame."

"Allie, move!" Mom grabbed my arm, yanked me back as Samarek's hand swiped through the space where I'd been standing. "We need to close it. Now."

"How?" Daddy was already moving, putting himself between me and the portal. "Her blood didn't work before. We tried—"

"It has to be blood," Zane said, his face pale but determined. "With my father, it's always blood."

"We tried that before," I said. "My blood. It did nothing."

"You tried it alone," Zane said, and that's when I understood.

"We're both a vessel that's been shadowed," I said. "Blood flowing but tainted by a demon."

"My blood, too, then," Mom said.

"And mine," Zane said. "And yours," he added, nodding to Daddy.

"On three," Mom said, pulling out her knife as Samarek snarled and leaped, appendages and wings bursting out, but its bulk still trapped—though I knew it could break through any moment.

"Hurry!" I said, as Mom counted, "One. Two. Three."

As one, we used our blades, sliced our palms, then let the blood flow onto the door.

"Blood, freely given," Zane murmured as Samarek snarled and the ground shook and I feared the Safe Room would fall through the ceiling and squash us all.

"NO." Samarek's voice was a thunderclap. "You would betray your own father, boy? Your own blood?"

"You were never my father." Zane's voice shook, but he didn't back down. "You were just the thing that used my mother. The thing that made me into a weapon. I'm done being what you created. I'm choosing something else."

Then he went quiet. The glow on the door disappeared. The light around the frame faded. The portal collapsed in on itself, folding and twisting and shrinking until it was a point of light, a spark, nothing at all.

The floor became plain, boring concrete once again, with no portal in sight.

Samarek was gone.

We'd done it.

I sat back on my heels, breathing hard, staring at the empty space where a door to hell had been. Daddy was on his knees beside me, clutching his shoulder, blood seeping between his fingers. Zane was flat on his back, chest heaving, eyes fixed on the ceiling.

Mom bent her knees, pulled me into her arms so tight I couldn't breathe.

"You did it," she said.

"We did it," I corrected. "All of us."

I looked at Zane, still lying on the floor. He turned his head, met my eyes.

"We are who we choose to be," he said.

I smiled. "Yeah," I said. "That's right."

27

KATE

The silence after a battle is its own kind of loud.

We sat in the ruins of our common room and tried to remember how to breathe. The demons were gone. The portal was closed. Samarek was banished.

We'd won.

It didn't feel like winning.

Eric was beside me on the couch, his shoulder bandaged. The wound was deep but clean—it would heal. Everything would heal, eventually. That's what I kept telling myself.

Allie was curled up in one of the armchairs, Jared perched on the arm beside her, his hand resting on her shoulder like he was afraid she'd disappear if he let go. She hadn't said much since we'd come up from the basement. None of us had.

Zane sat apart from the group, near the window, staring out at the darkness. He'd barely spoken since the portal closed.

"And Timmy?"

Laura's voice broke through my fog. She was standing in the doorway, phone in hand.

"Mrs. Micari just checked in. They made it to Eddie's

shop. Timmy's asleep." She managed a tired smile. "Apparently he thinks the whole thing was a very exciting game."

Something in my chest unclenched. My baby was safe. Whatever else had happened tonight, my baby was safe.

"Mindy?"

"Shaken but fine. They'll be back soon. And Eliza's got the students outside. No major casualties. They're helping her do some sort of blessing for the house."

I nodded. "Good."

"Sophie had a panic attack, but she's breathing again." Laura crossed the room, picking her way through the debris, and sank down onto the floor beside the couch. "We lost some furniture. Some windows. A truly impressive amount of drywall." She paused. "We didn't lose anyone."

We didn't lose anyone.

And yet Trevor was still dead. Antonio was still dead. But tonight—this battle, this apocalypse that had been building since before I'd even known it was coming—we'd survived. All of us.

"It's over," Eric said quietly.

"The portal's gone." I leaned into him, let his arm wrap around me. "Samarek's back in whatever hell he crawled out of."

"So it's over."

"This part is."

Because that was the truth of this life, wasn't it? There was always another demon. Another threat. Another door that needed closing. But right now, in this moment, we had won. And that had to be enough.

I pushed myself up from the couch, crossed the room to where Zane was still sitting by the window. He didn't look up when I approached, but I saw his shoulders tense. I sat down on the windowsill beside him. Outside, the first hints of dawn were starting to lighten the sky. We'd been fighting all night.

"You hanging in there?"

"He was my father," Zane said. "I know he was a monster. I know he used me, manipulated me, turned me into a weapon. But he was still—" His voice cracked. "He was still the only family I had."

"That's not true." I put my hand on his arm. "Not anymore."

He stared at me.

"You did good tonight. You helped close the portal even though it meant destroying your own father." I squeezed his arm. "That makes you family, Zane. Whether you want it or not."

For a long moment, he didn't say anything. Then something in his face crumpled, and he was crying, ugly, heaving sobs that shook his whole body. I pulled him into my arms and held him while he fell apart, this boy who had been raised as a weapon and had chosen to become something else.

"It's okay," I murmured. "You're okay. You're one of us now."

Across the room, I caught Eric's eye. He was watching us with an expression I couldn't quite read. Then he nodded, just once, and I knew he understood.

We'd started this night as a school full of hunters and students and broken people trying to hold the darkness at bay.

We'd ended it as a family.

It wasn't perfect. It wasn't pretty. But it was ours.

And right now, that was enough.

EPILOGUE
ALLIE

Two weeks later, the house almost looked normal again.

The windows had been replaced. The furniture had been repaired or swapped out. The bloodstains had been scrubbed from the floors, and the holes in the walls patched and painted.

If you didn't know what had happened here, you'd never guess that this had been the site of an apocalypse.

But we knew. We'd always know.

Jared and I were sitting on the balcony off the training room when I heard them. Mom and Daddy walking across the back lawn toward the cemetery.

I probably should have let them know we were there, but the truth was that I liked watching them. They felt right together, and my frequent calls to Stuart assured me he had no hard feelings. I was talking to him now.

"She's wearing her wedding ring again," I told him. "Daddy's. But on her right hand."

"I'm glad they're together," Stuart said. "They deserve to

be happy after what those two have been through. And I have a feeling that ring will move to her left hand soon."

"Is that a step-dad thing or an oracle thing?"

He just laughed. "Guess we'll see."

"For that matter, you already knew she was wearing it again, didn't you?"

He chuckled. "I take the Fifth."

"Are you okay with it? Mom and Daddy?"

"I am," he said firmly. "I'm truly happy for them. Also happy that you're all coming to Rome next month. Don't tell your mother I gave you a heads up. She hasn't even told me yet."

I laughed. "That's great. Timmy's going to be thrilled."

"Don't tell him at all. I trust you to act surprised. Your little brother? Not so much."

I promised I would, gave him Jared's love, too, then ended the call and snuggled up on the porch swing with Jared as we watched the sunset.

Later—much later—we lay tangled together in my sheets, moonlight pooling across the bed.

"I could stay like this forever," Jared murmured against my hair.

"Forever's a long time."

"I'm immortal. I've got nothing but time."

I wanted to tell him I was thinking about that, too. About spending time—all the time—with him.

But I wasn't ready yet. Maybe I never would be. But that was okay. Right now, I was happy, content in the arms of the man I loved. Tomorrow there'd be new adventures, new challenges. Tonight, there was just me and Jared.

Eternity could wait for when I was ready.

Who knows? Maybe someday, I would be.

THE END

ABOUT THE AUTHOR

J. Kenner (aka Julie Kenner) is the *New York Times*, *USA Today*, *Publishers Weekly*, *Wall Street Journal* and #1 International bestselling author of over one hundred novels, novellas and short stories in a variety of genres.

JK has been praised by *Publishers Weekly* as an author with a "flair for dialogue and eccentric characterizations" and by *RT Bookclub* for having "cornered the market on sinfully attractive, dominant antiheroes and the women who swoon for them." A six-time finalist for Romance Writers of America's prestigious RITA award, JK took home the first RITA trophy awarded in the category of erotic romance in 2014 for her novel, *Claim Me* (book 2 of her Stark Saga) and another RITA trophy for *Wicked Dirty* in the same category in 2017.

In her previous career as an attorney, JK worked as a lawyer in Southern California and Texas. She currently lives in Central Texas, with her husband, two daughters, and two rather spastic cats.

Stay in touch! Text JKenner to 21000 to subscribe to JK's text alerts.

J. Kenner Facebook Page
Facebook Fan Group
Join JK's Elite Reader Group!

www.jkenner.com

OLIVERHEBERBOOKS

A small press bound by the belief that every voice matters.

Sign up for our newsletter to learn about new releases and
more.
https://oliver-heberbooks.com/subscribe/

Follow us on social media:

facebook.com/oliverheberbooks

instagram.com/oliverheberbooks

amazon.com/oliverheberbooks

youtube.com/@OliverHeberBooksPublisher

www.ingramcontent.com/pod-product-compliance
Lightning Source LLC
Chambersburg PA
CBHW020335180726
47991CB00020B/1700